STORIES
FROM HANS CHRISTIAN
ANDERSEN

BLITZ EDITION

The Ugly Duckling

It was summer! The wheat was yellow as gold, the oats green and the meadows were dotted with fragrant haystacks.

There were green woods all around the fields and meadows, and in the woods, magnificent deep lakes.

How wonderful the country was!

An old castle with a deep moat around it was glittering in the sun. Along the old castle walls grew gigantic vines, all intertwined and almost as wild as those which were found in the woods.

At the foot of the wall, tucked in the thick, lush foliage, a duck was sitting on her nest.

The duck was quacking impatiently for she found that it was all taking too much time. Her eggs should have been hatched by now! Also, she was in a bad mood because hardly anybody ever came to visit her. She was looking reproachfully at the other ducks who would rather swim in the castle moat than come and have a little chat with her.

Then at last, the eggs began to crack!

"Peep! Peep!" – one by one, little heads came poking through the eggs. "Crack! Crack!" – the shells broke open and the ducklings worked their way out of the eggs.

The young ducklings nudged each other and looked with astonishment upon this bright new world.

"Peep, peep, this new world is so big," said the ducklings, for in the nest, they had a lot more room than in the egg.

"If you think that this is the whole world, you are quite mistaken," said Mother Duck. "The world is a lot bigger than that. It contains the whole garden of the castle and stretches all the way into the parson's field. And that is so far away that even I have never set foot there."

Then Mother Duck stood up and

"My, what a big boy we have here," said Mother Duck.

said "Are you all here now? Yes? No, not all! The biggest egg has not opened yet. Aw, aw, how long will I have to wait. . . I am running out of patience." And so, she returned to her egg.

"Good morning Mrs. Duck, how are you today?" asked an old duck who came to see how she was getting along.

"Ah, my dear friend, this one egg here just will not crack open. I do not understand at all. But have a look at my other little ones. Aren't they wonderful? Though I must say, it is a pity that they should look so much like their father, who has left me here all alone. Can you believe that he has not come to see me even once!"

Let me have a look at that egg," said the old duck. "I could almost bet that we have a turkey's egg there. They tricked me once that way too, and let me tell you, I had such a hard time with those little ones! Try what I might, they absolutely refused to go into the water. Well, let me see that egg! Yes, oh yes! That's what I thought, a turkey's egg. You don't need to bother sitting on that one, for you'll only have problems with turkeys. Your time would be better spent teaching your own brood how to swim!"

"Well, I shall give it a try," said

Mother Duck. I have held out so long, a few more days won't matter."

"You must know best," said the old duck and went away.

At last, the big egg burst open.

"Peep, peep," said the little one as he stuck out his head.

"Crack, crack, plunk!" – what was that? The shell had broken in two and the young one fell to the ground with a thump. Mother Duck looked quite puzzled, for it was really a very large duckling!

"My, what a big boy we have here," she said. "But he is definitely different from the others. Maybe he really is a turkey. One way or another I shall soon find out, for even if I have to throw him in myself, he shall go into the water!"

The next day, the weather was splendid! The sun shone brightly and warmed the water of the moat. Mother Duck called all her ducklings together and said, "Come along, children, today we shall go swimming."

She led them to the moat. One by one, the ducklings jumped into the water.

They went "peep, peep" as they disappeared head first under the water.

And so, the duck family entered the duckyard.

They were a bit startled, and, when they came to the surface again, they began to peep excitedly and swim in little circles. But they quickly realized that they were able to float on the water, whether or not they moved their little feet. And so they swam around for a while. And the big duck, who was the last to come out of his egg, was swimming along with them.

"You see, he is definitely not a turkey," said Mother Duck. "Just look how well he swims, and how gracefully he holds his head! He is my boy, no doubt about it! Actually, the longer I look at him, the more handsome I find him. Quack, quack! Come with me children, I shall show you the world now, and introduce you to the other animals. Be sure to stay close to me and beware of the cat! You understand?"

And so, the duck family entered the duckyard. There was quite a commotion going on inside. Two duck families were fighting over a fish head. But in the end, neither side got to enjoy the morsel, for the cat ran away with it!

"Did you see that, children? That is the way of the world," said Mother Duck.

6

She gave the cat a look, for she too would have liked to have a bite of the fish head.

"Now I want you all to go pay your respects to that old duck over there," she continued. "She is the most respected duck in the whole duckyard, because of her Spanish blood. That is why she is so fat. And do you see that red rag tied to her leg? Well, it is the highest distinction a duck can receive. It means that she is in charge here! Go ahead, move on! And watch your step! No, don't turn in your toes. A well-bred duck sets his feet well apart, like this! Then you bow nicely and say: Quack! Quack"

The ducklings went and did exactly as their mother had told them. But all the ducks and hens in the yard laughed at them, saying "What are all these ducklings doing here? As if we weren't crowded enough in this yard

All the ducks began to peck him.

already. Ugh! Just look at that one! What's that ridiculous thing doing here? We don't want to be seen near such an eyesore! Out with him!"

And a big duck pounced on him and bit him on the neck.

"Leave him alone, he is not bothering anyone!" said angry Mother Duck.

"But he looks so ridiculous. He is ugly and much too big!" said the duck who had bitten him.

"However, your other children are all sweet little things," said the Spanish duck with the red rag on her leg. "Except for that misfit. Maybe you can do him over?"

"I'm afraid not, Your Highness," said Mother Duck. "He may not be as good looking as the other ducklings, but he certainly is the sweetest of them all. And he is such a good swimmer, I'm convinced that everything will turn out all right. He will grow smaller eventually. I think the trouble is that he stayed inside the egg too long."

She looked at her ugly little Boy and smoothed his feathers lovingly.

"What is more," she continued, "he is a little boy, not a girl. So his looks aren't that important after all. And anyway, I think he is quite a fine fellow. He can take care of himself."

"Well, your other children are little darlings, you know," said the Spanish duck once again as she looked at each of them carefully. "Do make yourselves at home now. And if you should happen to find a fish head somewhere, make sure to bring it to me."

"Hurray," cried the ducklings as

they went off to play. They frolicked and had so much fun, it was a pleasure to see them.

But the ugly duckling, who was truly too big for a duckling, was not allowed to join in the games. He was pecked and tormented by all the ducks and hens in the yard.

"He is much too big for our yard," said a chicken, who in turn was much too small.

"Pooh, how ugly he is!" said a haughty duck.

And a turkey, who imagined himself to be the lord of the yard, gobbled loudly and with his tail spread wide, jumped straight at the poor duckling. Planted in front of him, the turkey blew himself up until he was huge and round and his head became flaming-red. The ugly duckling became so terribly frightened that he ran to hide somewhere. He sat in a corner, feeling dejected because he was so ugly and because nobody found him even a little nice to be with.

That is how life began for our ugly duckling.

In the days that followed, the duckling was bothered even more than the first day. Even his little brothers and sisters began to tease him, saying, "We don't want to be your brothers

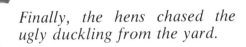

Finally, the hens chased the ugly duckling from the yard.

and sisters anymore. You are much too ugly. We hope that you get eaten up by the cat. You clumsy fool!"

Even his own mother wished not to see him anymore. She said: "If only he could go somewhere far away from here!"

After that, all the ducks began to peck him and the hens chased him and bit him wherever they could.

So the duckling ran away from the

He came upon a great marsh where a big flock of wild ducks lived.

yard. He ran so hard that the little birds scurried from the shrubs. "They run away from me because they find me ugly too," sobbed the duckling.

He came upon a great marsh where a big flock of wild ducks lived. There, the duckling lay down, exhausted. He was so very tired and so desperate!

10

The following morning, when the wild ducks woke up, they were surprised to see this ugly duckling who had ventured into their territory. "Who are you and where do you come from?" they asked. The duckling greeted them all, left and right, as nicely and politely as he knew how.

"Oh, but how ugly you are!" said the ducks. "You may stay here, but only if you promise to leave our young girls alone."

Poor ugly duckling! He was so far from thinking of girls. All he wanted was a little kindness. He was only too happy to be allowed to stay in the marsh and drink its water.

The duckling had been in the marsh for two days, when two geese happened to fly overhead. They were two ganders actually, and they called to him "Hey there, below! You are so ugly, my friend, that we can't help liking you. If you want, you can become a migratory bird, like us. There is another marsh, not too far from here. A few very sweet geese live there and we know that they too will find you loveable. So, how about coming along with us?"

A huge hunting dog appeared in front of him.

The duckling came upon a little farmhouse.

Suddenly, "Bang! Bang!" And the two ganders fell dead into the marsh.

Then again, "Bang! Bang!" And whole flocks of wild geese flew up from the rushes. The shots rang again and again. The hunters were all over the marsh. Some of them had even climbed the trees and were shooting the birds from above. Blue smoke rose up and hung above the water, and the water became dark red with blood.

Then came the hunting dogs. The whole marsh was rustling. The ugly duckling was terrified. He was just going to bury his head under his wing when a huge dog appeared right on top of him. His tongue was hanging and his eyes were glittering fiercely. He lowered his head towards the duckling. Then he opened his jaws. . . bared his pointed teeth. . . and snapped, but he did not touch the duckling.

"Good heavens," gasped the duckling, "I am so ugly that even a dog is too disgusted to eat me."

Shots echoed all over and the volleys whistled past the duckling on all sides. All the time he lay dead-still.

Late in the afternoon, the marsh finally became calm again. However, the duckling waited for quite a while before he dared to move. Then, very cautiously, he turned his head to the right, then to the left. He made sure that all was safe, then he dashed out of the marsh, as fast as his legs would carry him.

He raced up and down hills and over fields and meadows.

Meanwhile, a strong wind started to blow and the duckling had to fight his way against it. But he went on running.

It was already getting dark when he came upon a farmhouse. The little cottage was so dilapidated, it looked as if it stood only because it did not know which way to fall.

It started to rain and the wind blew even harder. The ugly duckling looked around the house. He saw a crack in the front door, just big enough to let him squeeze through. And that's exactly what he did!

An old woman lived in the cottage with a cat and a hen. The cat's name was Bossy. He could arch his back, and he could also purr. The hen was called Shortie, because she had such little legs. She laid very nice eggs, and that is why the old woman loved her hen so much.

The cat and the hen both noticed the duckling at once, and the cat arched his back high while the hen cackled.

"What's the matter with you both?" asked he woman and looked around the room. She had poor eyesight and she took our duckling for a big wet duck sitting in the corner of the room.

"That must be a stray duck. What a find," she said. "Now I shall enjoy some duck eggs also. I only hope that it's not a drake. But we shall soon find out."

Three weeks went by, then four weeks. But of course, there were no eggs.

The cat and the hen considered themselves very important. At least ten times a day they would say "We and the world!" For they thought that they were as important as half the world, and the better half of the world at that.

13

The ugly duckling did not agree with them. He said that the world was actually quite different. But the hen did not want to hear any of it and she became indignant.

"Tell me, can you lay eggs?" she asked angrily.

"No, I can't", said the duckling.

"Then will you please shut your big mouth!"

And the cat said "Can you maybe arch your back or purr?"

"No, I can't" said the duckling.

"Then you don't even have the right to disagree. That means that you have to keep your mouth shut when those who know better are talking."

The duckling went and slouched dejectedly in a corner of the room. He thought of the fresh air and the warm sunshine, and of a blue pond. Suddenly, he felt an irresistible urge to go outside and splash around in the water.

It was a feeling so strong, that he could not keep it to himself, so he told the hen.

"You are a strange beast indeed!" said the hen. "It is all because you don't do a thing all day. Why don't you lay an egg or arch your back, and you'll feel normal again."

"But it is so marvelous to be in the water! You can duck your head, and even dive all the way to the bottom.

"Now you are really talking nonsense! What do you mean, marvelous? You must be mad! Why don't you ask the cat what he thinks of ducking his head in the water? Or ask the old

"What a find," said the woman.

woman. How do you think she would like to get her head all wet?"

"Ah, you don't understand a thing about it. . ." sighed the ugly duckling.

"Well, if we don't understand, who else could possibly understand? I hope that you don't imagine yourself to be cleverer than the cat or the woman, not to mention myself. Oh my, where are your manners? You are a terrible bore and I really don't enjoy your company! But I would like to help you. So you must believe me when I tell you that everything will be all right if you only try to learn how to lay eggs and purr."

"I still think that I should go out into the wide world," said the duckling.

15

At sunset, a whole flock of marvelous white swans came down from the sky.

"That is the wisest thing I have ever heard you say," answered the hen.

And so, the duckling went away.

For a whole week, he did nothing but glide on the water, duck his head and dive down to the bottom. But there was nobody to play with him because he was so ugly.

And then came fall! The leaves on the trees became yellow and brown. The wind played with them and spun them off the branches. The air grew cold and the clouds gathered above, filled with hail and snow. A raven, sitting on a fence, croaked:

"Everybody's co-old! Aw, aw, everybody's sooo co-old!'

And the ugly duckling was cold too! Very, very cold!

One evening, as the sun was slowly disappearing behind the woods, a whole flock of marvelous white birds came down from the sky. They had the strangest voices, and long, slender necks, and wonderful white wings.

They were swans, on their way to warm places far away, but of course, our duckling did not know that. He could not take his eyes off the big beautiful birds. After they had rested for a while, they spread their wings again and flew off, far away from the cold.

The duckling gazed at the swans until they were no more than little dots on the horizon. He felt happy and sad at the same time. Where did these marvelous birds come from, and where were they going to?

Yet, the duckling was not at all en-

16

The duckling felt happy and sad at the same time.

The farmer saw the duckling lying there and freed him from the ice.

vious of the beautiful birds. He never thought of wishing anything so unbelievable for himself. He was happy enough that they had done him no harm when they had gone past him.

Poor ugly, young duckling!

Winter came, a very cold winter too. It was freezing. The little duckling had to keep swimming round and round in the water to keep himself from freezing. But the circle in which he swam was becoming smaller and smaller every night. The duckling went on swimming until he keeled over with exhaustion and was frozen solid in the ice. Just at that moment, a farmer came along. He saw the duckling lying there and freed him from the ice. The farmer tucked him under his thick jacket and took him home. From the heat of the stove, the duckling came back to life.

The farmer's children wanted to play with the duckling but he thought that

The children wanted to play with the duckling but he thought that they were going to hurt him.

they were going to hurt him. He got so terribly scared that he jumped in panic and landed in the milk bucket. The milk splattered all over. The farmer's wife shouted and clapped her hands. The duckling flew out of the milk bucket and into the butter tub, out of the butter tub, and into the flour bin.

20

The duckling rushed out of the house.

Oh, Oh, what a mess the duckling made!

The farmer's wife was still shouting and trying to chase him out of the room with the broom. The children were jumping excitedly and screaming with laughter. They were climbing over each other to catch the duckling.

Luckily, the door was open. The duckling rushed out of the house and into the snow. He ran until he could run no more, and fell asleep in a thick bush. . .

Fortunately for our duckling, the cold did not get much worse. And he was able to find a little food, so that he made it through the long winter.

Finally, at long last, spring was

The duckling lay down in a thick bush.

here! The duckling felt the rays of the sun getting warmer. What a joy it was to hear the little birds twittering in the rushes.

The duckling stretched his wings. They had become large and strong. Before he realized what was happening, he was flying high and landed in a big garden. There were apple trees in bloom and graceful lilacs, all the way down to a blue lake.

Everything was so magnificent, and the fragrance of the lilacs was so sweet!

Suddenly, three beautiful white birds came swimming from behind the bushes. They were large, with slender necks and wonderful white wings.

Their feathers rustled softly as they slid majestically across the water. The duckling recognized the white birds, for they were the same ones he had seen the previous fall. He had felt both sad and happy then, but this time he only felt sad.

"How I would love to go meet those beautiful birds," thought the duckling. "But I don't have the courage, they are sure to peck me to death for being so ugly. . . Still, I would rather be pecked to death by the beautiful white birds than to be pestered again all summer by ducks and hens. . ."

Finally, spring was here. The duckling stretched his wings.

And without further hesitation, the duckling jumped into the water and headed towards the swans. When they noticed him, the swans began to flap their wings with surprise. Full of curiosity they started to swim towards him.

"It's all right, you can pick me to

What did the duckling see in the clear water of the lake?

The swans gathered around him.

death," said the ugly duckling as he bowed his head down to the water. "I'd rather have you. . ."

But what did he see in the clear water of the lake? It was no ugly, grey duckling but a wonderful white swan. "I'm a beautiful swan too! I'm a beautiful swan too!" he cried with delight. The swans gathered around him and stroked him with their beaks and their white wings. He was so happy now, after all the the grief he had endured.

Some children came running through the garden. They threw pieces of bread and grain into the water. The smallest one shouted,

"Look, there is a new swan in the lake. How lovely!"

"Yes, yes," the other children began to shout. "How nice it is to have a new swan in the lake." And the children clapped their hands and danced around singing "A new swan, a new swan!"

They went to fetch their mother and father. More pieces of bread were thrown into the lake. And all the children were saying,

"The new swan is the most beautiful. Oh, how handsome he is!"

Then all the other swans bowed to the young swan. It made the young swan so embarrassed that he hid his head under his wing. But he felt so happy inside! He thought of all the times when he was being tormented and chased away from everywhere. Oh, how much sorrow he had gone through! And now, everybody was only saying the nicest things to him.

The young swan stretched his slender neck.

The lilacs bent their branches even further over the water towards him. And the sun caressed his shiny white feathers. He stretched his slender, long neck, he rustled his feathers and rejoiced with all his heart.

"I could never have dreamed of so much happiness when I was still only an ugly duckling!"

28

The Steadfast Tin Soldier

Once upon a time there were twenty-five tin soldiers. They had all been made from one large tin spoon and were all brothers. How they had actually been made, not a soul in the world could tell.

Only the moon knew all about it for she had seen it all. There she stood, in the sky, full and round, among thousands of stars that filled the night, and she watched the old tinsmith at his work until the late hours.

During the day, the old man had to work very hard to earn the twenty pennies on which he lived. Even in those days, it was very little money but luckily, he was very thrifty, so he was able to survive on those wages. During the day, he repaired leaking copper faucets and lead pipes, but at night, after he finished his meal of brown bean soup and his pudding, he set off to make toys!

The moon with her round face, looked through the attic window and saw how the tinsmith started by breaking an old tin spoon into three pieces. He threw the pieces into a big iron ladle and melted them in the furnace. The moon noticed that the old man had prepared twenty five molds and put them on the side. Every mold had a small opening on top of it, and when the tin had melted, the tinsmith took a little funnel and carefully filled each mold with the liquid metal.

From the dark evening skies, the face of the full moon watched intently. What was going to happen next? But the moon will have to wait some more before finding out, for that night, nothing happened at all! The old man put down his iron smelting ladle and closed the furnace door. He was totally unaware that the moon had been looking over his shoulder all along.

"Look at this, it is already past eleven," the tinsmith muttered, "and tomorrow is another early day." He blew out the candle and went to bed. The full round moon was left out there, waiting and peering through the window. She was so very eager to see what would come out of the twenty five little molds. All night long she stood there, but by the time the old man woke up the next day, the sun was just coming up. And everyone knows, of course, that the sun and the moon never stay together in the sky. They actually relieve each other, like guards. So, when the old tinsmith got up with the sun, the moon had to go to bed, for her time was up. Now she would have to hold her curiosity until the evening.

That day, the tinsmith worked particularly hard in order to earn his brown bean soup and his pudding. He had quite a few jobs to finish and all the repairs were needed urgently!

When he finished his dinner and shuffled over to his furnace, the moon was already at her post. Her full round face was bursting with curiosity! The old man took the first mold into his hands.

The moon heard the hinges squeak softly. The mold opened, and. . . the old man was holding a tin soldier in his hand, a little soldier complete with a gun over his shoulder!

But that wasn't all! One more tin soldier came out of the next mold and the next, and so on. . . . until there were altogether twenty-five soldiers. The old man went to sit on a little wooden bench by the table. He took a little paintbrush and, with a few strokes, he gave the soldiers a red jacket and blue pants.

They looked so splendid now, his twenty-five tin soldiers. The old man said to himself with a sigh of satisfaction,

"If I manage to sell them to the toy shop tomorrow, they will bring at least thirty pennies. I shall then be

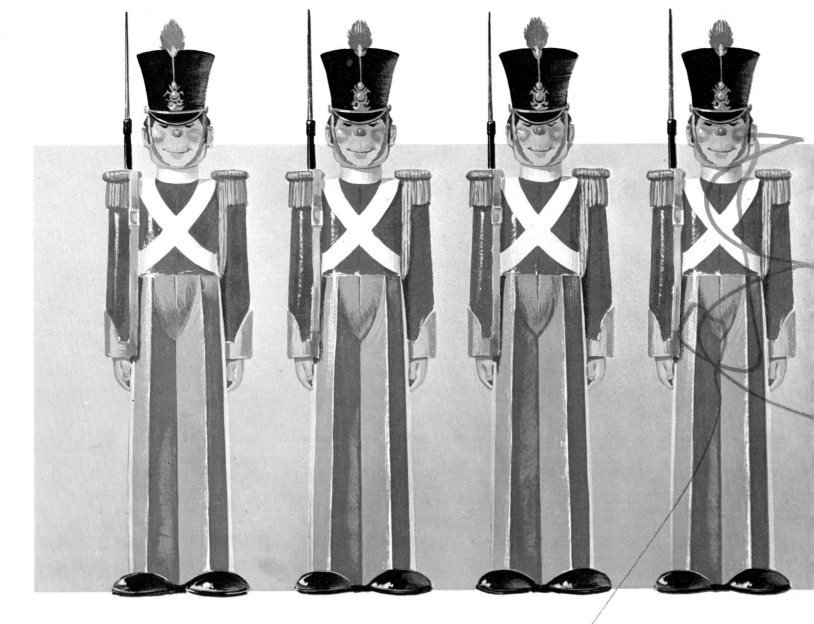

How splendid the tin soldiers looked!

able to buy a pretty doll for my granddaughter whose birthday will be in two days."

And the moon. . . didn't say a thing. She was so impressed by the tinsmith's craftmanship that she shrank back in awe! The following night, there was nothing left of the moon but a thin cresent, high up in the sky.

"It's the new moon tonight," people said. But that was not correct, it was still the same old moon and it was going to take almost a whole month before her face becomes full again.

And what happened to the tin soldiers in their nice blue and red uni-forms? The owner of the toy shop bought them and arranged them in a pretty box. That very afternoon, an Army general came into the toy shop. He wore a uniform almost as elegant as that of the soldiers, but not quite so new and bright.

"I want to buy a little present" he said to the shopkeeper. My grandson has his birthday tomorrow. Do you have a beautiful toy for him?

The owner of the toy shop looked at the imposing uniform his customer wore. There was a real general indeed!

31

"I have something very special for you!" he said. "Something particularly suited for the grandson of a general. I have these beautiful tin soldiers. How do you like these?"

"Tin soldiers! Oh, how splendid!" answered the general. "I'll take them."

The most beautiful present of all was a cardboard castle.

32

When the general's grandson opened the box on his birthday, he said exactly the same words, "Tin soldiers! Oh, how splendid!" He always tried to imitate his grandfather!

The boy immediately arranged the soldiers in a row on the table, all twenty-five of them. The soldiers all looked alike, except for one of them who had only one leg. He was the last one to be cast and unfortunately, the tin had run out. But although he only had one leg, he was as steadfast on it as the other soldiers who stood on two legs. He is just the one we are going to hear about, for all kinds of adventures are going to happen to him!

There were many more toys on the table where the birthday boy had arranged his soldiers. All were toys he had received for his birthday from his mother, his father, his aunts and uncles, and from his little cousins. He had even received all kinds of presents from a soldier who served under the general and who would love to become sergeant, and from a sergeant who wanted to become a captain, also from a captain who wanted to be a general but who would never dare admit it.

That is how it always goes in the world. A general is a very important person and he receives presents from a lot of people when members of his family have their birthday.

The general's grandson had a whole

A piece of silver foil was glued to the green field and represented a lake.

table loaded with new toys. The most beautiful toy of all was a big cardboard castle, complete with lots of towers and walls and gates. There was even a flag waving from the highest tower, it was white with a gold crown in the center. Quite a marvelous castle indeed! The towers were all covered with gold foil, the gates opened and closed and there was a real drawbridge with real chains. One could even see through the windows into the

A pretty girl stood by the castle gate.

richly decorated rooms where paper dolls were sitting on gilded armchairs and sky blue couches, just like real people.

Around the castle there were gardens with green cardboard trees and brightly painted flower beds. A piece of silver foil was glued on a green field, it represented a lake. Swans were swimming in it and their image was reflected in the silvery water. It was altogether a very exciting toy.

A very pretty girl stood by the castle gate. The tin soldier tried not to stare but he could not keep his eyes off her. She wore a lacy skirt and a blue scarf around her shoulders, and on her scarf, a shiny little pin. The girl was a ballerina and she held her arms up above her head, while her left leg was pulled up under her skirt. To the tin soldier, it seemed that she had only one leg, just like himself.

"There is the perfect wife for me!" He said to himself. "Only, she is much too fancy for me. She lives in a magnificent castle and I live in a box, and it is not even all mine, all twenty-five of us sleep there! That is not sort of home one can offer a lady. But I say, a soldier has to be steadfast. I don't care how I do it or how long it takes, I shall have to make her acquaintance!"

He stood on his toes and made himself as tall as possible, so that he could watch her over the tobacco box that stood in front of him on the table. He kept staring at the ballerina who was able to stand on one foot all this time without losing her balance for an instant.

Evening came. The other twenty-four tin soldiers came running to the box from all sides of the table. They had enjoyed themselves very much all day. Before they went to sleep in their box, they told each other how each of them had spent the day. Some had thrown bread crusts to the swans in the lake and others had stood guard in the gardens of the castle. A couple had been lowering and lifting the drawbridge to let various guests in and out. And all of them had admired the pretty ballerina. Soldiers will always be soldiers, even if they are made of thin!

"Only, a simple soldier shouldn't even look at such a fancy lady." said one of them. "I, for instance, have met a simple peasant girl instead. I met her down in the green fields and she even allowed me to kiss her."

The others were a little envious of his success, but the one-legged soldier thought,

"You have it your way and meet anyone you want. But I shall get to know the ballerina if it is the last thing I do on this earth!"

After the tin soldiers and all the other toys on the table had gone to sleep, the people of the house went to bed also, for it was already ten o'clock.

But two hours later, when the little clock under the glass bell struck twelve, all the toys woke up, as if by magic. You see, toys don't look like they are alive while the children play with them. But at night, everything changes. At the stroke of midnight, all the toys jump up and run off to play. They play at visiting each other or at making war, or sometimes they have a party and they dance. . . .

The tin soldiers in their box were making an unbelievable noise because they could not push the lid open.

In the meantime, the acrobat doll was already tumbling over and over and the slate pencil was writing jokes all over the slate. The commotion was such that even the canary in his cage woke up and started to sing.

The only two who remained quiet were the ballerina and the tin soldier. After the other tin soldiers in the box had gone to sleep, the steadfast tin soldier had marched off in the direction of the tobacco box. He had stood there stiffly and stared at the ballerina, convinced that she would soon notice him and that they would become friends.

But the ballerina did not even look in his direction. She just stood there, with her arms up in the air, poised on the toes of her one foot like a model soldier.

And that is how they still were now, when all the others were having fun. At the stroke of midnight, the lid of the tobacco box suddenly sprung open. But there was not even a pinch of tobacco in the box. Actually, it only looked like a tobacco box, but wasn't really one. It was a jack-in-the-box the children liked to use to scare people. So the lid sprung open with a plop and a little imp shot out.

"Hey you, tin Soldier!" cried the imp with a shrill voice. "Will you stop staring at that girl already!"

But the tin soldier was much too steadfast to be startled. He just pretended not to hear.

The tin soldier positioned himself by the tobacco box and kept staring at the ballerina.

"Don't you hear me?" screamed the angry imp. "I'm telling you to stop staring at that girl like that! What are you doing here anyhow? You don't even belong here, you are supposed to be in the box with all your brothers. Just listen to the noise they are all making! What a rowdy bunch of brutes you soldiers are! Get away from here!" But the steadfast tin soldier stood his ground bravely.

"All right, just you wait then. To-

"All right then, just you wait! Tomorrow you will be sorry!" threatened the imp.

morrow you will be sorry!" And with that threat the imp curled back into his box and slammed the lid shut.

The tin soldier stood at attention all night, watching the beautiful ballerina.

He was still determined to get to know her, however difficult it may turn out to be!

The next day, the children found him still standing there, next to the tobacco box which wasn't a tobacco box.

"The other soldiers are all sleepy-heads," said the little boy whose birthday was now over. "They are still lying in their box. But this one here is the true soldier! I shall have him stand guard on the windowsill. He will make sure that nobody sneaks in through the window."

The little boy took the tin soldier and placed him on the windowsill. And now, whether it was the imp's threat come true or just a draft, nobody will ever know. In any case, the window suddenly flew open and the little tin soldier fell from the third floor all the way to the pavement outside!

Suddenly the window flew open and the soldier fell out.

39

The bayonet of his rifle was impaled between two paving stones.

40

First, it felt like he was falling for ever. Then he felt a shock and found himself lying upside down in the street. The bayonet of his rifle was impaled between two paving stones, and a steadfast tin soldier never lets go of his weapon, however uncomfortable he may be.

The little boy and his brothers and sisters hurried down the stairs. Even the maid ran behind them to help them look for the lost soldier. They looked all over and they did not find him. A few times they passed so close by the little soldier that he feared that they would step on him.

Of course, the tin soldier could easily have cried to them, "Here I am!" But he didn't think it proper for a soldier to shout while in uniform.

It started to rain. A few drops to begin with, then harder and harder and within a few minutes, it was a real downpour. The water ran down the sidewalk and streamed into the gutter. After the rain had stopped, two little street boys came by.

"Look what I found!" said the older one. "A tin soldier. We can play with him and make him float in the gutter!"

They found an old newspaper that was still dry and folded it to make a boat. Then they put the soldier in it and let the stream carry it down the gutter. The little boat gathered speed and the boys ran along with it, clapping their hands in excitement.

Oh dear! The rain water was rushing so fast and the waves shook and

They looked all over and they did not find him.

tossed the fragile boat about. What a turmoil! No wonder, it had been a heavy downpour and there was a lot of water everywhere.

The little boat was still thrown about by the torrent, it rocked back and forth and leaned dangerously. At times, it became caught in a whirl and swung about so wildly that the tin soldier staggered. But he didn't allow

The boat went down into the sewer.

"Let me see your passport!" said the rat.

himself to be scared at all. He still stood there, straight and stiff, staring ahead as if nothing had happened.

The boat went down into the sewer. Suddenly, everything became completely dark around the soldier.

"Where shall I end up?" he asked himself. "Of course, it is that awful imp who put me in this mess because I was staring at the ballerina. Ah, if only I had her here with me on the boat, I wouldn't care if this place were ten times darker! But it is no fun at all being here all alone."

The tin soldier was a real soldier, and like any soldier, he still thought of his pretty girl, even in the greatest of dangers.

No, there was no pretty girl where he was now, just a big disgusting rat, who lived in an underground cave and sprang out of the darkness at the tin soldier.

"Go away, rat!" shouted the soldier. "Can't you see that I have a loaded weapon on my shoulder?"

"How dare you speak to me in such a way!" answered the rat haughtily. "Can't you see that I am a border inspector? What you just said is an offense to an officer on duty. I am writing you up! Speak, what is your name

43

and rank? Your rank, I said! You mean you don't even have a rank? So, you are just an ordinary soldier."

The soldier looked straight ahead and did not say a word.

"You must have a passport?" asked the rat. "Let me see your passport!"

But the soldier still refused to say a word. He just held his gun tighter to his side. Just then, the little boat was caught in another whirl, and carried off. The rat was left there, jumping up and down and baring his ugly teeth as he snarled, "Stop the soldier, Hold him! He is crossing the border and he does not even have a passport!"

The stream was becoming stronger and carried him even faster down the sewer. Eventually, the tin soldier thought that he saw a little spot of daylight in the distance.

But what was that at the end of the tunnel? Suddenly, there was a rumbling, a terrible roar, enough to scare even the bravest soldier. The water was surging into a wild river. Can you imagine how terribly frightening it was for the poor tin soldier, even a steadfast one like ours! Just think how you would feel if you were falling down a waterfall as high as a house, and then if you were thrown all the way into the deep sea!

The little soldier was so close to the waterfall that there was nothing more he could do to save himself.

Then, he stood up to his neck in water.

However, in spite of it all, the tin soldier still remained steadfast! Not a muscle twitched in his face. In spite of all the danger, he still stood as stiff and straight as ever. He was getting closer and closer to the big waterfall and there was nothing he could do to stop the boat now.

Finally, he was thrown into the deep. But he still stood up. He didn't even blink an eye!

The little boat started to spin. Water rushed in over the side and filled the boat to the rim. At last, it had to sink.

The tin soldier felt the water rising. First to his knees, then to his waist, and soon he was standing in the water up to his neck. The boat sank deeper and deeper through the waves. The newspaper was soaking wet and started to fall apart. The water rose and began to tickle the soldier's nose. Then a wave rolled over his head. Only the tip of his bayonet still showed above the surface of the water. . .

The tin soldier was thinking of the lovely ballerina whom he would never see again. He thought that there was a voice whispering in his ear, "Danger, danger, steadfast soldier! Death is coming near!"

Then the paper bottom of the boat finally caved in and the soldier fell through. High above him, through the murky water, he could see the blue sky. And deep underneath him, in the half darkness of the sea, there were all

45

towards him, but it was no train. It was a big fish, and the soldier, who had never been near the water before, did not know what a fish was. He had never seen one before, not even a tiny little fish, let alone an enormous one like this.

The fish opened its enormous mouth!

kinds of strange aquatic plants. The little soldier was sinking quickly, because he was heavy, like all tin soldiers. There was a strange shadow looming in the distance. What could it be? An enormous monster, with eyes as big as train lights! It was swimming

The fish was at least twenty times as big as the tin soldier and his eyes glistened hungrily.

,,No, I am not going to get scared now." Thought the tin soldier. He tried hard to stay as stiff as possible, and all the time, he was sinking deeper and deeper towards the bottom of the sea. He clasped his rifle close to his body and looked straight ahead.

But if our little soldier thought that seeing mean, vicious eyes was the worst thing that could happen to a tin soldier under water, he was wrong, because what happened to him next was much worse!

The fish opened its enormous mouth! All around him, the tin soldier saw a row of tiny white, needle sharp teeth. He did his best not to blink his eyes, for he had to remain steadfast. But it was too terrible a sight. He couldn't stand it anymore and finally had to close his eyes. He felt sucked by a very strong current. And. . . he disappeared into the mouth of the monster fish!

The cook cut the fish open with a big knife.

How dark it was in there! It was much darker than in the sewer and very tight. But, in spite of everything, the tin soldier remained steadfast and did his best not to show his fear.

After swallowing our poor soldier, the fish still went on swimming in search of food, because a tiny soldier was not enough to satisfy his hunger, even if the tin snack now lay heavy on his stomach. He swallowed some small fish and some shrimp and then he also gulped down a worm that was wriggling invitingly at the end of a line.

The soldier found himself in the same room where he had been unpacked the day of the birthday party.

48

it was taken into a kitchen to be prepared. The cook used a big knife to open the belly of the fish.

At last, after what seemed to be a long, long time, the tin soldier saw daylight again. Everything was bright around him again, and he could hear the cook exclaiming, "Look what I found here, a tin soldier!"

She picked him up, and, holding him with two fingers, she took him into the living room. Everyone wanted to see the funny little man that had been found in the belly of the fish they were going to eat for dinner! The tin soldier was not very happy to be shown around like that, he felt he had nothing to be particularly proud about.

They put him on a table and.... how strange life can be sometimes... the tin soldier realized that he stood in the very same room where he had been unpacked at the birthday party!

The same children stood all around him and the same toys were still on the table! He saw the tobacco box which was not a real tobacco box, and the tumbling acrobat. He saw the slate pencil that had been writing jokes on the slate, and he recognized the magnificent castle. The swans were still swimming in the sparkling lake. The flag with the crown still waved from the highest tower. The cardboard dolls still sat on the gilded armchairs and the sky blue sofas. And by the gate stood a ballerina with her arms stretched out towards the sky. And she still stood balanced on one leg.

But that turned out to be a mistake, for suddenly the fish felt a terrible pain in his mouth as it was being yanked up through the water. The fish twisted and turned and tried to shake itself free, but nothing helped. Inside, in its belly, the tin soldier was getting sick from all the commotion.

But things calmed down soon, and then, all was completely still.

After it was caught, the fish was brought to the market and sold. Then,

The tin soldier was so overcome with emotion that he almost started to cry. But he bit his lip, for it wouldn't suit a steadfast soldier to stand there and cry. He looked straight at the ballerina and she looked straight at him and neither said a word. . .

And then, something very strange happened.

Suddenly, the little brother of the boy who had received the toys on his birthday grabbed the one-legged tin soldier and threw him into the fire. Just like that, without saying a word.

The tin soldier was blinded by the flames and extremely hot. But he wasn't sure if it came from the fire or because he was so in love with the ballerina. The bright colors of his uniform were licked away by the flames. . . He felt that he was beginning to melt, but he still

Like a feather, she flew into the fireplace, and landed right in the arms of the tin soldier.

remained steadfast. He still had his gun on his shoulder. He would never let go of his gun. . .

At that instant, somebody opened the living room door. A draft lifted the ballerina and she flew like a feather into the fire, right into the soldier's arms. She was made of cardboard and instantly went up in flames. In a few seconds, she had completely vanished. The tin soldier had never been happier. He had held her in his arms for an instant and now he was satisfied and he could melt away.

The next morning, when the maid came to clean the ashes from the fireplace, she found a shapeless lump of tin. Nothing remained of the ballerina, just her charred little pin among the ashes.

The maid found a little lump of tin and a black pin among the ashes.

51

The Flowers of Little Ida

"Why are my flowers looking so sad?" asked little Ida.

"Ooh, my flowers are almost dead," said little Ida. "Only last night they were still so beautiful and now they are all faded and their leaves are drooping. I wonder why that could be?" she asked the young student who was sitting on the couch. He was her tutor and she found him very sweet and liked him because he always told her the nicest stories. And he also cut funny figures out of paper, like a heart with dancing girls all around it, and flowers, and castles with a gate that you can actually open and close.

"Tell me, why are my flowers looking so sad?" little Ida asked once again, and showed him the vase where a bunch of flowers were wilting away.

"Don't you know what happened?" asked the student. "Your flowers have gone to the ball last night and they danced so much that they are completely exhausted now. That is why they let their heads all hang down."

"But flowers cannot dance!" said little Ida.

"What do you mean 'flowers cannot dance'! Of course they can!" said the student. "At night, when it gets dark and we are all asleep, the flowers jump out of their vases and their pots and run around the room. Every night they have a ball."

Little Ida looked at him with big puzzled eyes.

"Are children allowed at the ball, too?"

"Of course they are! The flowers bring their own children along. Their children are the little daisies and the lilies of the valley."

"And can you tell me where do all the most precious flowers hold their balls?" asked little Ida.

"Well, have you ever been to the big palace where the king spends his summers? You must have seen his magnificent garden, that is filled with all kinds of marvelous flowers in summer. And remember the white swans, how they come gliding on the water and stretch their graceful necks when you throw bread for them into the pond? You can be sure that there is always a ball going on in that palace!"

"Only yesterday, my mother took me there for a walk," said little Ida. "But the trees had lost almost all their leaves and all the flowers were gone. Where do you think they went? There were so many of them all summer long!"

"They are all inside the palace," said the student. "As soon as the king and his court moved back to the city for the winter months, the flowers made themselves at home inside the palace and started celebrating. If only you could see those parties! The two most splendid roses jump up on the throne and pretend to be the king and queen. And surrounding the throne, there are rows and rows of cockscombs, standing proud and tall, as soldiers of the royal guard are supposed to. Then, all the nicest, sweetest, prettiest flowers make their entrance, and the dance begins. The blue violets are all young officers and they dance with the hyacinths, and the crocuses,

The two most beautiful roses go
to sit on the throne and
pretend to be the king and queen.

who are all duchesses. The tulips and the portly lilies are respectable elderly ladies who keep a sharp eye on the dancers, to make sure that they behave properly and do not step on each other's stems."

"And the king doesn't mind if the flowers live in his palace while he's away?" asked Ida. "Doesn't anybody throw them out when they see them dancing all over the palace?"

"Nobody knows they are there, not even the king," said the student. "Once it happened that the old watchman came into the ballroom to make sure that everything was all right. Fortunately, he carries a big key chain, loaded with keys that jingle as he walks, and they made so much noise that the flowers heard him before he came in and scrambled for cover. Some hid behind drapes and others huddled in a corner. "What is

going on here," said the watchman. "I could swear that I smell flowers. Hmm, that is strange. . . ." He looked around and sniffed the air, but he never found anything suspicious, so he decided that it must have been his imagination.

"I'm so glad he didn't catch them!" said little Ida and clapped her hands. "Do you think that I could get to see the flowers sometime?"

"But of course!" said the student. "Next time, when you go for a walk in the garden of the palace, go to one

Once it happened that the old watchman came to see if every-thing was all right.

I'm so glad he didn't catch them!" said little Ida and clapped her hands.

of the windows, but don't make any noise, and take a peek inside. You may well see a flower or two. I just went by there this morning, and I saw a big yellow lily sleeping on the couch, stretched out like a duchess! She was probably pretending to be a real duchess or a lady-in-waiting of the queen."

"How about the flowers in the professor's garden, do you think they could go to the ball too? But how could they walk so far?"

"Easy," said the student. If they

want, they can even fly! You must have seen the pretty red and yellow butterflies that look just like flowers? Well, that's exactly what they are, flying flowers. All they have to do is shake themselves loose of their stalks and take off. They flap their petals as if they were wings and they fly high up in the air. Whenever they have been good, they don't have to stay on their stalks, and they can spend the whole day flying about like butterflies. When they stretch out their colorful petals, they fill the air with their fragrance, and all the gardens are bright with flowers that look like butterflies and with butterflies that look like flowers, all gaily fluttering about. I'm sure you saw them too.!"

Little Ida nooded.

The student went on, "I'm afraid, it is possible that the flowers in the professor's garden have never had a chance to go to the palace, and don't even know what fun they can have there every night. I have an idea, we could play a little joke on the professor, you know how fond he is of his flowers and how he fusses over them all day!"

"Yes, let's play a joke on the professor!" exclaimed little Ida and clapped her hands excitedly.

"Listen, tomorrow, when you walk through his garden, you must tell all the flowers that there is a ball at the palace, the flowers will spread the word around, and as soon as the sun goes down, every single one of them will fly off to the palace. So when the professor comes out to have a last look at his dear flowers before going to bed, there will not be a single tiny little flower left anywhere! Can you imagine how amazed he will be! I can already see him running up and down

"What a funny story!" exclaimed Ida and laughed.

his garden with his arms up in the air!

"But how can the flowers spread the word about the ball? Everybody knows that flowers cannot speak!"

"Flowers do not speak, it's true, but they can make gestures. Didn't you ever see how a flower nods its head and moves its leaves, and sways back and forth in the breeze? That is the language of flowers. To them, all these gestures are as clear and easy to understand as our language is to us."

"And what about the professor? Do you think that he can understand their language too?" asked little Ida.

"Some of it, yes. One morning for instance, he went out to the garden, and came upon a big nettle who was speaking in flower language to a pretty red carnation. The professor understood that the nettle was saying, "You are very beautiful and I love you so much!" But the professor did not like the idea of one of his carnations falling in love with an ordinary nettle, so when he realized what the nettle was saying, he immediately went to pull it out, but as soon as he touched it, the nettle burned his hand like a flame. Now, he doesn't even come close any-

"There you are again, telling all kinds of nonsense to this child!" said the dull neighbor.

Ida placed the little flowers in the doll's bed and covered them.

"Now you must be good little flowers and lie there and rest," said Ida to her flowers.

Little Ida went to the window and looked at her mother's healthy flowers.

more and the nettle and the carnation have become the best of friends."

"What a funny story," said little Ida, laughing.

"There you are again, telling all kinds of nonsense to this child." said the neighbor who had just dropped in and was sitting on the sofa. He was a dull young man who didn't like stories at all. He didn't like our student either and he always said the most disagreeable things to annoy him. When the student was cutting little figures out of paper, the neighbor told him that it was a silly waste of time. The student didn't care about the neighbor's opinion, he just went on cutting his figures, and Ida had never seen anyone so skillful. Do you know that once he had even cut a little man

hanging from a gallows and holding a heart in his hands.

"Why do you think this man was hanged?" he had asked. "He was hanged because he was a thief. He stole somebody's heart!"

Another time, he cut out an ugly witch riding on a broom.

The neighbor must have been jealous of the student because he was too clumsy and could never cut all those complicated figures, and, as we said, he was too dull to be able to tell any stories.

"You shouldn't be telling this child all that stuff and nonsense," said the neighbor once again. "It is completely ridiculous!"

But little Ida was fascinated by everything that the student told her about the flowers and she spent a lot of time thinking about it. So that's what it was then: when the flowers hang their heads, it is simply because they are tired from having danced all night. Who would have believed it?

Ida took her flowers into her playroom. There was a chest of drawers where she kept all her beautiful toys, and by the chest, a little bed where Ida's doll, Sophie, was asleep.

"I'm sorry, little Sophie, you will have to get up now! Tonight you are sleeping in the drawer, I'm afraid. We shall have to give your bed to these poor little flowers. They are almost dead of exhaustion and they will have to rest here until they get better. But don't you worry, by tomorrow they ought to be completely recovered."

The doll was not at all happy with the arrangement and she just lay there pouting, but Ida paid no attention to her. She took her out of her bed and put her in a drawer.

Then she gently arranged all the little flowers on the soft pillow and covered them with Sophies yellow blanket to keep them nice and warm. She told them that they had to be good little flowers and lie there quietly and rest. She was going to make them some herb tea to help them get their strength back. She promised them that tomorrow she would allow them to get up again. Then she drew the bed curtains and tiptoed out of the room.

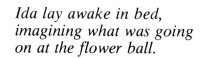

Ida lay awake in bed, imagining what was going on at the flower ball.

All evening long she thought about all the many flower stories the student had told her, and before she went to bed she looked at the window box filled with her mother's bright red geraniums. How fresh and healthy they looked compared to her own pitiful bunch!

She winked at them. "I know that you are ready to go dancing tonight. . ." she whispered. But the flowers pretended not to hear. They just stood there looking pretty and did not stir a leaf.

Ida lay awake in bed, imagining what was going on at the flower ball. Oh, how she would love to see all the flowers dancing at the king's palace!

"My own little flowers would certainly have liked to be there, but they are much too weak to go dancing tonight!"

Eventually, she fell asleep. But a short while later, she woke up again. She had dreamed of the flowers and of the student and of the boring neighbor who had said that it was all nonsense.

All was quiet in the house. Her mother and father were asleep, and the only light came from the little night lamp on her bedside table.

"I wonder if my flowers are still lying in Sophie's bed?" she whispered. "I'm so curious! maybe they were naughty and went to the palace anyway?" She sat up in bed and tried to look into the playroom, whose door had been left open. All her toys were there, sleeping, and she could see Sophie's little bed with the curtains

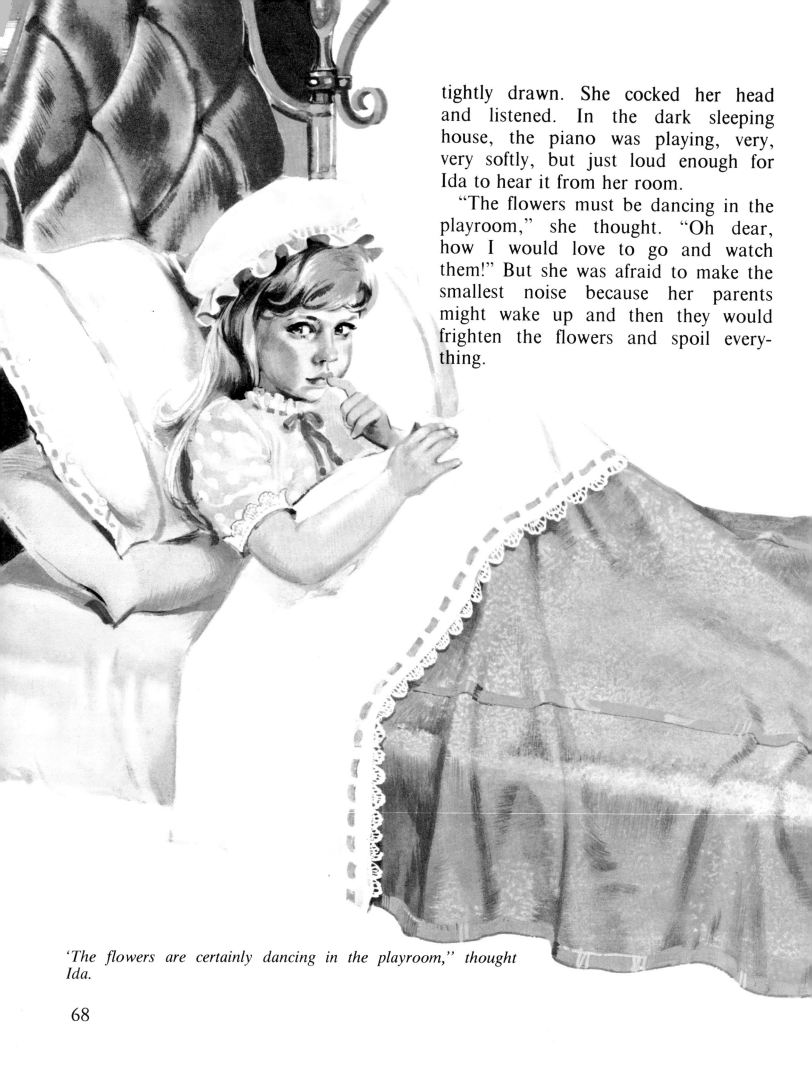

tightly drawn. She cocked her head and listened. In the dark sleeping house, the piano was playing, very, very softly, but just loud enough for Ida to hear it from her room.

"The flowers must be dancing in the playroom," she thought. "Oh dear, how I would love to go and watch them!" But she was afraid to make the smallest noise because her parents might wake up and then they would frighten the flowers and spoil everything.

'The flowers are certainly dancing in the playroom,'' thought Ida.

"Maybe if I'm patient, they will come and dance in my room too," she thought. "That would be marvelous!"

So she sat there and waited, but the flowers did not come and the soft eerie music still filled the night. Finally, little Ida could not resist the temptation any more. She had to get up, for she had never heard such heavenly music. Very carefully, she slid out of bed and tiptoed to the door.

The moon was shining through the window and the whole room was lit by a silvery glow. Ida could see as clearly as if ten candles were burning, and what an extraordinary sight it was! All the window boxes and flowerpots and vases were empty. The flowers were on the floor and they were having the time of their lives,

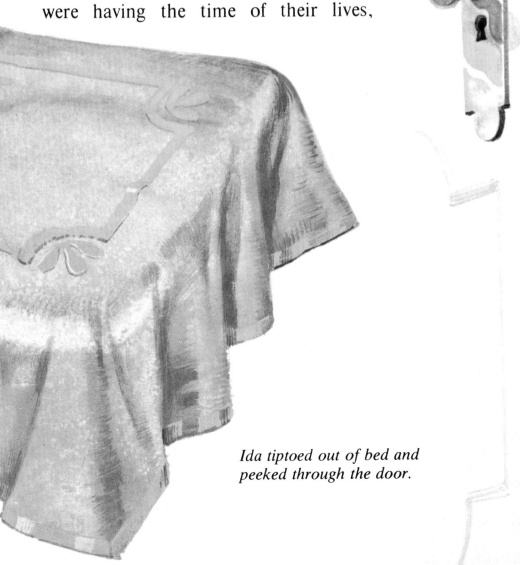

Ida tiptoed out of bed and peeked through the door.

dancing in a big circle, and whirling and leaping around. Then, they stretched their green leaves and swayed to the soft music, holding on to each other.

A big, beautiful lily was playing on the piano. Little Ida was sure that she had already seen that lily somewhere before. A few weeks ago, before the summer was over, she and her cousins were walking with the student and they saw a big yellow lily. She remembered the student saying, "Look at this lily, children, don't you think that she looks very much like Miss Line?"

Everybody had laughed, but Ida

The flowers were having the time of their lives, dancing in a big circle.

thought that the long yellow lily looked exactly like their nursemaid, with her long thin neck and her yellowish complexion. They even looked alike when they played the

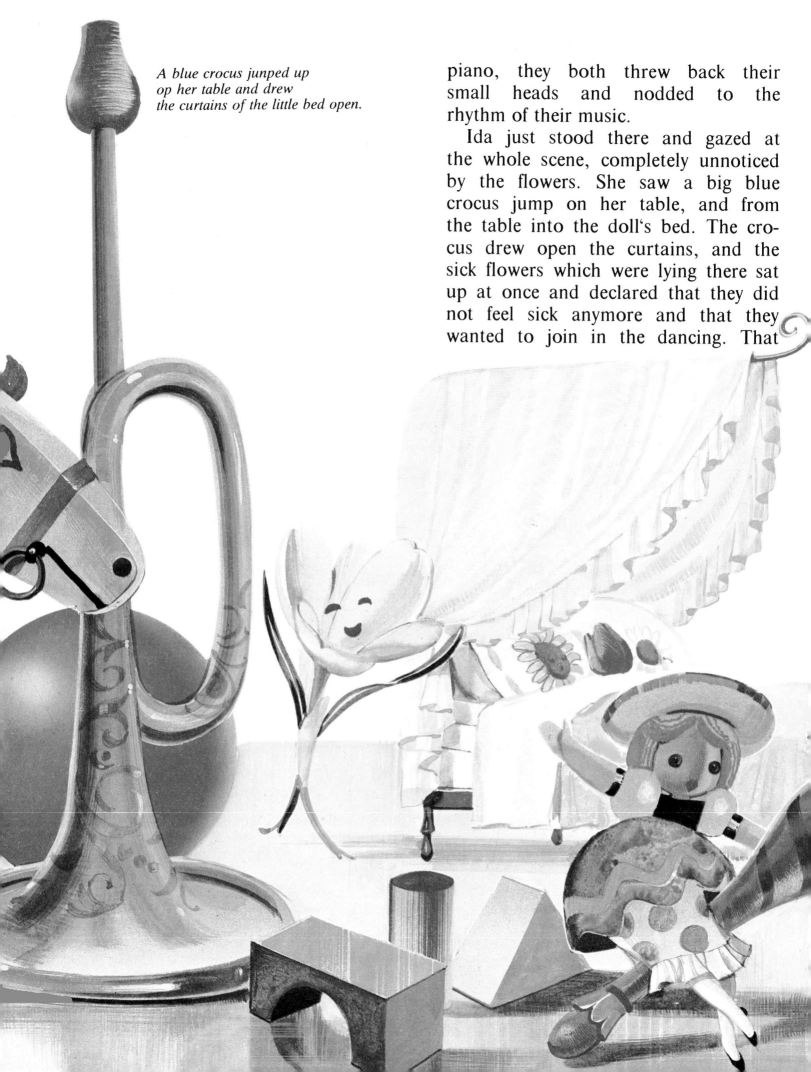

*A blue crocus junped up
op her table and drew
the curtains of the little bed open.*

piano, they both threw back their small heads and nodded to the rhythm of their music.

Ida just stood there and gazed at the whole scene, completely unnoticed by the flowers. She saw a big blue crocus jump on her table, and from the table into the doll's bed. The crocus drew open the curtains, and the sick flowers which were lying there sat up at once and declared that they did not feel sick anymore and that they wanted to join in the dancing. That was true, they did not look sick at all anymore. Their stalks were strong again and their petals were bright and they sprung from their beds and hurried to greet the other flowers.

Suddenly, there was a crash, as if something had fallen off the table. Ida looked around, and indeed, it was the carnival staff that had jumped down to the floor. The night before was Mardi Gras and the staff was still wearing his fancy carnival decorations: a red ribbon and red and yellow tassels, and he felt handsome enough to dance with the flowers.

He even danced the mazurka and jumped up and down and stamped his one wooden foot.

The flowers had never seen such a lively dance and they could not join him, for they were too light and dainty to be stamping their feet.

Then suddenly, the carnival staff started to grow! He grew and grew, till he became a big tall puppet. He started turning round and round and shouted, "Is it all ridiculous, why do you tell all that stuff and nonsense to the poor child?"

Ida couldn't believe her eyes: the carnival staff had a face just like the young neighbor who came to visit that morning. Finally, the bow and tassels gave him an angry look and muttered something. The big puppet blushed with embarrassment and shrank down

The carnival staff danced like mad, stamping his wooden foot.

The flowers had to ask the carnival staff to be a little more careful.

till it became just the right size for a carnival staff again.

Ida found the whole scene very funny and couldn't help laughing out loud.

The staff couldn't keep still and started to dance again, the tassel and the red ribbon had no choice but to bounce along, whether they wanted to or not. This time, the staff got so carried away that the poor ribbon almost came off.

Now, Ida's flowers had to ask him to be careful and he stopped dancing for a while.

There was another noise, from the toy chest this time, and all the flowers stopped to listen. It was Sophie, who had been sleeping in the drawer and was knocking and crying to be left out. The staff leaped up on the table and pulled and pushed and somehow managed to pry open the drawer.

Can you imagine how amazed Sophie was when she poked her head out of the drawer and saw the merry scene in her own playroom! She rubbed her eyes, thinking that she was maybe still dreaming. But the scene did not go away! Finally she asked, "Am I dreaming or is there a ball going on here? And why wasn't I invited? You should have woken me up!"

The staff came up to her and asked, "Will you dance with me, dear Sophie?"

"Dance with you, never! You are too ordinary to be my dancing partner," said Sophie and turned her head away.

"Is there a ball going on here?"

She sat there in her drawer, hoping that one of the flowers would ask her to dance at last. But they left her all alone. She made all kinds of little noises to draw their attention, and she coughed a few times: ahem, ahem!

But still, nobody seemed to care about her, and the carnival staff was out there, dancing all by himself.

Finally she got so mad that nobody noticed her, that she let herself fall down from the drawer and crash down to the floor. She managed to make so much noise, that now everybody noticed her.

Oh, what a confusion! All the flowers rushed to see if she was hurt. They surrounded her and wanted to make sure that she was all right. They were all so very friendly, especially the ones who had slept in her bed.

They told her that they were little Ida's flowers, and they thanked her for letting them use her bed. They said that they had slept very well and that it had helped them get better again. To show how grateful they were, they took her to the center of the room, in the pool of bright moonlight, and all the flowers made a circle and danced around her.

How happy Sophie was! She was so

75

touched by all the concern, that she even said to the flowers that they could keep her bed forever and that she didn't mind at all sleeping in her drawer.

The flowers said, "That is very kind of you, dear Sophie, but we won't need your bed anymore because we are not going to live much longer. By tomorrow we shall be dead. Can you please tell little Ida that she should bury us in the garden near the spot where she buried her canary. But she should not cry because we shall come back next year and we shall even be more beautiful than we are now.

"Oh, no! Please, you must not die! Do you hear me!" exclaimed little Ida. She ran into the playroom and kissed her little flowers tenderly. But just at that moment, the other door of the room opened. A whole row of magnificent flowers came dancing in.

Ida had no idea where they could be coming from. She guessed that they must be the flowers from the royal pal-

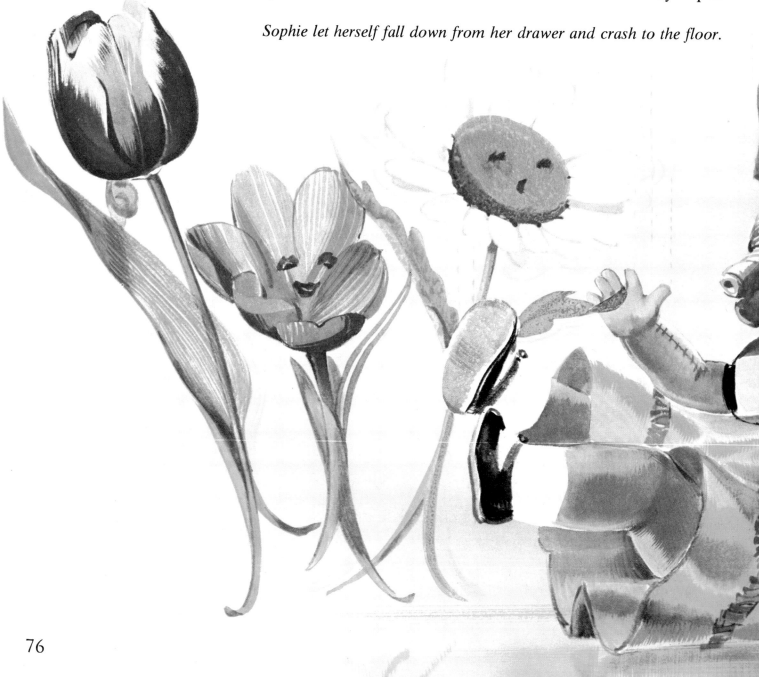

Sophie let herself fall down from her drawer and crash to the floor.

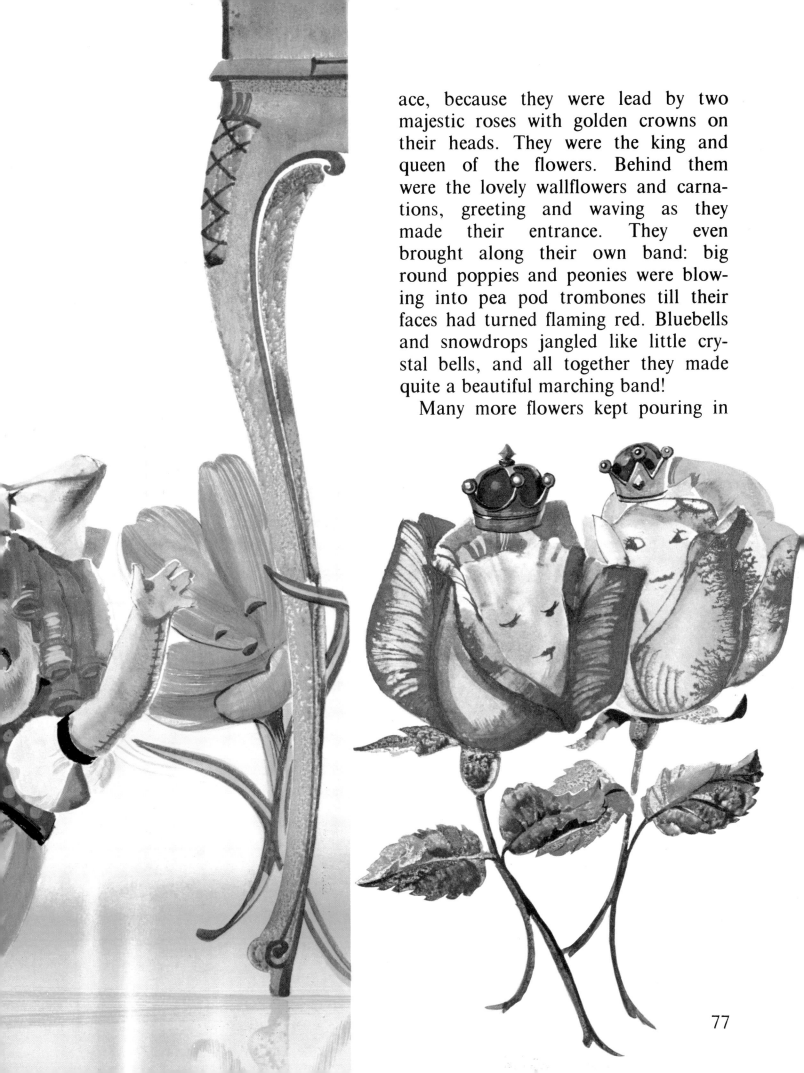

ace, because they were lead by two majestic roses with golden crowns on their heads. They were the king and queen of the flowers. Behind them were the lovely wallflowers and carnations, greeting and waving as they made their entrance. They even brought along their own band: big round poppies and peonies were blowing into pea pod trombones till their faces had turned flaming red. Bluebells and snowdrops jangled like little crystal bells, and all together they made quite a beautiful marching band!

Many more flowers kept pouring in

and they all danced and spread their fragrance in the room that was already getting crowded. There were blue violets and pink daisies, asters and lilies of the valley and all were so happy to be together that they hugged and kissed each other and gave a lovely ballet performance.

When the moon went down, the ball drew to an end, the flowers all wished each other a good night and little Ida went back to bed.

The next morning, as soon as she woke up, she ran to her doll's bed to see if her flowers were still there. Carefully she opened the curtains. . . and they were there all right, but they were all withered and in much worse shape than yesterday.

As for Sophie, she was still in the

Jonas and Adolf shot their arrows in the air.

drawer where Ida had put her the day before. But how sleepy she looked!

"What fun we had last night, didn't we Sophie?" said little Ida. But Sophie just stared ahead and said nothing.

"What's the matter with you this morning, why are you in such a bad mood? Didn't everybody dance with you last night?"

Her little flowers were dead and Ida promised to bury them in the garden, so that they should come next year. She found a cardboard box decorated with pictures of birds, opened it and put the flowers inside.

"My cousins will be here soon and they will help me bury you near the canary, as you had asked. Till next year then, dear little flowers. I do hope that you will come back even lovelier than this year."

Ida's cousins were two very strong young boys. Their names were Jonas and Adolf.

All three children went down to the garden to bury Ida's flowers. Jonas and Adolf had brought along their bows, and arrows which they had just received from their father, and Ida carried the box with the flowers.

Before Ida laid the box down, she kissed her flowers one last time. Then Jonas and Adolf shot their arrows in the air, just like the real soldiers shoot their cannons and their guns when a general is being buried.

Thumbelina

Once upon a time there was a woman who wanted very much to have a child.

One day she went to see an old witch and asked, "I want to have a child so badly. Can you tell me what I should do to have one at last?"

"If you really want it, it will be possible!" said the witch. "Here is a grain of corn. It is not the same sort of corn that is found in the fields or used to feed the chickens. This is special corn. Just plant it in a flowerpot and you shall see!"

"Thank you very much," said the woman and gave the witch twelve pennies for her trouble. The woman went home and planted the grain of corn in a flowerpot. Soon the grain sprouted. Whithin a few days, a big beautiful flower appeared. It looked like a tulip bud, with its petals tightly closed.

"What a lovely flower," said the woman, and she kissed the soft red petals. At that instant, the bud opened with a soft pop. In the heart of the flower, sitting on its green pistil, was a sweet little girl, no bigger than a thumb. So, the woman called her Thumbelina.

She gave Thumbelina a varnished nutshell for a bed, blue violets for her little mattress, and rose petals for her blanket. At night, Thumbelina slept in her nutshell and during the day she played on the table. There, the woman had arranged a dish filled with water, and flowers all around. A large tulip petal floated in the middle of the dish.

In the heart of the flower sat a little girl, no bigger than a thumb.

At night, Thumbelina slept in the nutshell.

Thumbelina sat on the petal and sailed from one end of the dish to the other. She used two white horsehairs to row with. What a joy it was to see her frolick on the water!

Thumbelina could also sing. Her little voice was so sweet that the woman's eyes filled with tears listening to her.

One night, as Thumbelina was sleeping in her little bed, a giant toad jumped in through the window. It jumped on the table where Thumbelina was asleep, dreaming of red rose petals.

"She would be a very good wife for my son!" said the toad to herself. She grabbed the nutshell in which Thumbelina was asleep and jumped back

The toad grabbed the nutshell in which Thumbelina was asleep and jumped through the window into the garden.

through the window and into the garden.

Nearby, there was a wide river, with marshy and muddy banks. The toad lived there with her son. He was ugly and coarse, very much like his mother, who had kipnapped Thumbelina.

"Croak, croak!" was all he said when he saw the pretty little girl in her nutshell.

"Don't be so loud, you'll wake her!" said the old toad. "She might escape, she's light as a feather. Do you know what we'll do? We are going to place her on a lily pad in the river. She is so tiny that it will look like an island to her and she won't be able to run

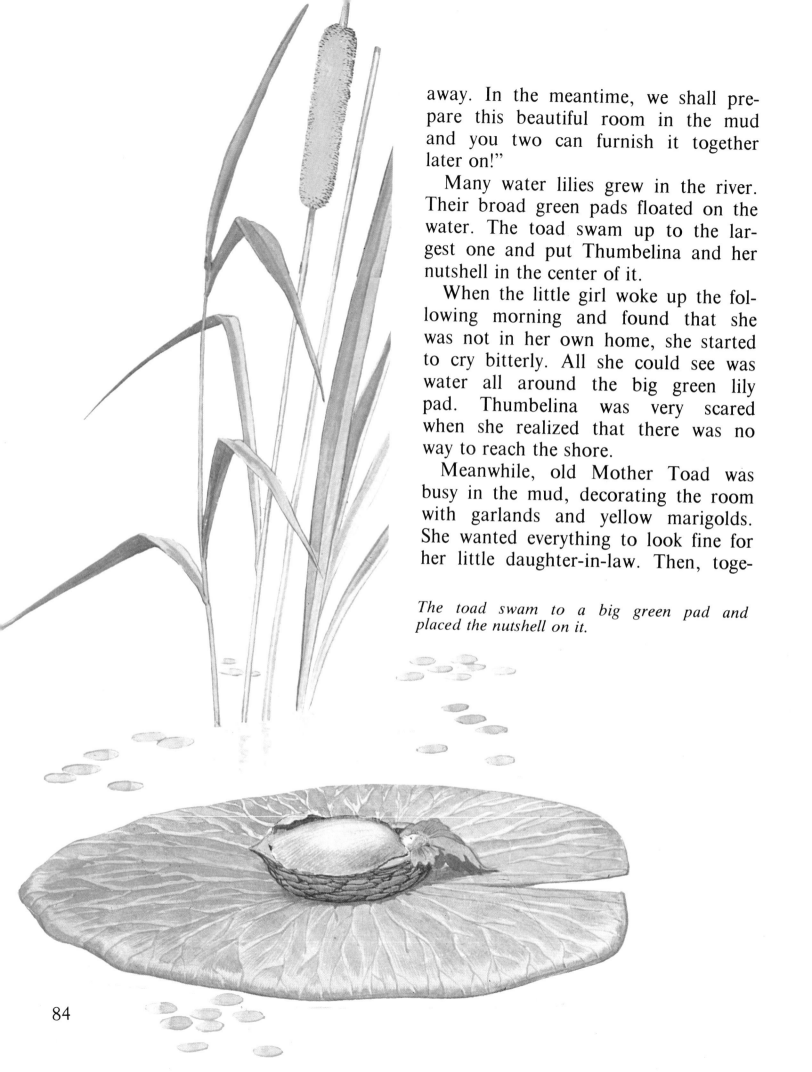

away. In the meantime, we shall prepare this beautiful room in the mud and you two can furnish it together later on!"

Many water lilies grew in the river. Their broad green pads floated on the water. The toad swam up to the largest one and put Thumbelina and her nutshell in the center of it.

When the little girl woke up the following morning and found that she was not in her own home, she started to cry bitterly. All she could see was water all around the big green lily pad. Thumbelina was very scared when she realized that there was no way to reach the shore.

Meanwhile, old Mother Toad was busy in the mud, decorating the room with garlands and yellow marigolds. She wanted everything to look fine for her little daughter-in-law. Then, toge-

The toad swam to a big green pad and placed the nutshell on it.

"Don't be so loud, you'll wake her!" said the old toad.

ther with her ugly son, she swam to the distant lily pad where Thumbelina was sitting. They went to fetch her beautiful little bed which had to be put into the bridal chamber before Thumbelina's arrival. Mother Toad bowed low before Thumbelina and said, "This is my son, and you are going to marry him. You will see how happy you will be with him in the mud!"

"Croak, croak!" said the son, for that was all he could ever say.

So they took her pretty little bed and swam away with it. And Thumbelina was once again all alone on the green lily pad. She cried, because she did not want to live in the mud with the old toad. And she definitely did not want to marry her horrible son!

The river was filled with all kinds of fish. They had seen and heard every-

Thumbelina cried because she did not want to marry the horrible toad.

Eventually, the pad drifted away, carrying Thumbelina down the river.

thing. They poked their heads high above the water in order to have a good look at the little girl. They all found her very lovely. What a pity it would be if she had to marry the ugly toad! No, that must not be, they decided! And they started to chew on the stalk of her lily pad. Eventually, the pad was cut off and, with Thumbelina, it drifted down the river. The cur-

Thumbelina spent all summer in the big forest.

rent carried it so fast, that the toad was not able to catch up with it.

Thumbelina drifted down the river for a long time. The little birds in the rushes alongside the river banks saw her and sang, "Look, look what a pretty little girl....!"

The pad was carried further and further down the river. When the current became weaker, the pad floated softly to one side. Cautiously, Thumbelina jumped onto the dry land. She looked all around and saw a big green forest in front of her. The most magnificent flowers were growing there and the birds were singing to their heart's delight. Thumbelina went to

live in the forest. She wove herself a bed from blades of grass and hung it under a big coltsfoot leaf, so that she would not get wet if it rained. She ate honey from the flowers and drank the morning dewdrops that covered the leaves.

Summer and fall went by. Then winter came. A long, cold winter. The birds, which had sung for her so beautifully, all flew away. The trees became bare and the flowers withered. The big coltsfoot under which she lived, shriveled away and nothing was left of it but a dry, yellow stalk.

Thumbelina became cold, very cold, for her clothes were all worn out by

When it rained, Thumbelina looked for shelter under a big leaf.

now. She was so frail and so small, that she would certainly freeze to death if the cold became much worse.

Then it started to snow. To her, every snowflake was as heavy as a shovelful of snow would be for us.

That is because we are big, and she was no bigger than a thumb. She tried to wrap herself in a dry leaf, but it didn't make her any warmer.

She left the forest where she had lived and came into a wheat field. But the wheat had long been harvested. Only the dry stumps were sticking from the frozen ground. For Thumbelina, it was like walking through a forest where all the trees had been cut off.

A beautiful winter butterfly fluttered around her and came to rest nearby. The butterfly was sorry that Thumbelina had to suffer so from the cold. He said that he would take her to a warm place where she could stay till summer came again.

Thumbelina was really very cold.

Thumbelina accepted his offer gladly. She fastened one end of her belt to the butterfly's waist and held the other end in her hands. But just as the butterfly was taking off, a big fat beetle came up to them.

As soon as he saw the pretty little girl, he grabbed her around the waist with his six legs and flew to the top of a tree with her.

Good heavens, how frightened Thumbelina was when the beetle put her down on a very high branch. But

she worried even more about the beautiful winter butterfly. He was now flying around with her belt hanging from his waist. It could get caught on a branch and he would starve to death.

The beetle couldn't care less. He put Thumbelina on the largest leaf he could find and fed her some honey. He told her how lovely she was and how she did not look at all like a beetle. Then all the other beetles who lived in the tree came to see her. They examined Thumbelina and found that she looked ridiculous. The female beetles touched her with their antennae and said, "Look, she only has two legs, that means that she cannot be very special."

"She doesn't even have antennae!" said another. "And her waist is so thin, ugh! She is just a human being!"

All the female beetles agreed that she was ugly. And yet, Thumbelina was so pretty! The beetle who had found her thought so too. But since all the others found her ugly, he changed his opinion and refused to have anything more to do with her! She could go wherever she wanted. So they took her down from the tree and left her on the freezing ground. Thumbelina sat there crying because she was so ugly that even the beetles did not want to keep her. Yet, she really was as lovely as you could imagine and as soft and fine as a rose petal.

Shivering with cold. Thumbelina ran back to the wheat field. She came

Thumbelina came upon the house of a field mouse.

upon the house of a field mouse. The door was hidden by wheat stumps. She knocked. The door opened, and inside. Thumbelina saw a plentiful supply of grain.

Poor Thumbelina stood humbly at the doorstep and begged for a grain of wheat for she hadn't eaten a thing in two days.

"You poor thing," said the field mouse kindly. "Come out of the cold and have something to eat."

And because Thumbelina had made a good impression on her, the field mouse later said,

"You can spend the winter with me, but, in exchange, you will have to take care of my house and tell me stories. I like stories a lot."

Thumbelina did everything the field mouse asked her to and she lived well in the house.

"We are soon going to have a visitor," said the field mouse after a few days. "My neighbor comes to see me once a week. His house is even more beautiful than mine and he wears a fancy fur coat. You would do very well for yourself if you decided to marry him. Only.... he is blind. So you will have to tell him the best stories you know."

But Thumbelina did not feel like marrying. And certainly not a neighbor and a mole at that! Anyway, he was coming to visit, in his black fur coat. The field mouse said that he was very wise and very rich. His house was at least twenty times as big as hers. Yes, he was wise indeed. But he did not care for flowers and sunshine. He said the worst things about them and had not even seen them.

Thumbelina had to sing for him. She sang "The Ladybug Song" and "The Wind in the Willows." The mole fell in love with her voice.... But he was old, and said nothing about his feelings.

He had dug a long underground tunnel. It went from his house, all the way to the field mouse's house. The field mouse and Thumbelina could walk in the tunnel as much as they liked, he said. He also said that they should not be afraid of the dead bird that was lying there. It was a little bird who had died from the cold a little while ago. It was buried just where the mole had dug his tunnel.

The mole put a rotting piece of wood in his mouth and lit it. It glowed in the dark. The mole walked ahead and lit up the long dark tunnel.

The mole had dug an underground tunnel.

When they reached the spot where the dead bird was buried, the mole pushed aside some earth to make way for them. And in doing so, he made a crack in the ceiling and let a ray of sunlight in. There, in the middle of the tunnel, Thumbelina saw a dead swallow. His pretty wings were pressed tightly against his body, he had buried his head in his feathers and pulled up his little legs. Thumbelina felt so sorry for the poor bird. She loved birds so much. All summer long, they had sung for her! But the mole only shoved the bird with his stumpy paw and said,

"This one won't be squeaking anymore! It must be awful to be born a bird. I am glad that my children do not look like that. All that birds can

Thumbelina saw a dead swallow lying there. His little wings were pressed tightly against his body.

do is "twitter, twitter" and when winter comes, they die from starvation!"

Thumbelina said nothing, but when the others had turned their back, she knelt by the bird. She smoothed the feathers on his head and kissed his closed eyes. "Maybe this is the very bird who sang for me so cheerfully all summer," she thought. "I wish he could know how much joy he has given me."

Then, the mole returned to fill the crack in the ceiling and walk the ladies back home.

But Thumbelina could not sleep that night. She got up and wove a warm blanket out of hay. She brought it down to the tunnel and spread it over the dead swallow. She had found some soft wool in the field mouse's house and tucked it on both sides of the little animal, to keep him from being too cold. "Farewell, my pretty little bird," she said. "Farewell, and thank you for having sung all summer for me, when the trees were still green and the sun kept us both warm."

She pressed her head against the little bird's chest. But she suddenly looked up, startled. It seemed that something was ticking inside. It had to be the little fellow's heart! The swallow was not completely dead! He had only fainted with cold. And now that he was being warmed, he was returning to life. It always happens that

The mole walked the field mouse and Thumbelina back home.

97

way. In fall, the swallows fly off to warm countries. And if some of them are delayed, they become so cold that they die and are covered by snow.

Thumbelina was trembling with fear. The bird was so big compared to her. But then, she got her courage back and tucked the wool even tighter around his body. She fetched the mint leaf that had been her blanket and covered the swallow's head.

The following night she slipped into the tunnel again. Now, the swallow was able to stand! But he was so exhausted that he only opened his eyes for a moment to show his gratefulness.

"Thank you kindly, my dear little girl," said the swallow. "I feel so marvelously warm now, and soon I shall be strong enough to fly away to the warm countries."

Thumbelina could not sleep that night.

"Oh, you must not do that," said Thumbelina. "It is still very cold outside. It is freezing and big snowflakes are falling. Just you stay in your warm little bed an I shall take care of you."

And she gave the swallow a little water from a flower petal. The swallow drank thirstily and told her how he had wounded his wing on a thorn. He hadn't been able to fly as fast as the other swallows who were leaving for warmer countries. He had become so exhausted that he had fallen. He could remember nothing after that, not even how he arrived in the tunnel.

Throughout the winter the swallow stayed in the mole' tunnel. Thumbelina was good to him and had grown quite fond of him. The mole and the field mouse never noticed anything for they did not pay attention to the swallow.

Spring came. And when the first rays of the sun warmed the earth, the swallow took leave of Thumbelina. Thumbelina opened up the gap in the mole's tunnel again. The sun came pouring in. The swallow asked if Thumbelina wanted to go outside with him. She could sit on his back and they would fly to the green forest. But Thumbelina knew that the field mouse

Throughout the long winter, the swallow stayed in the mole's tunnel.

would be sad if she left her so suddenly.

"No, I can't do that," she said. "Farewell, farewell! And good luck to you!"

"You are a good, sweet little girl," said the swallow and flew out to meet the sun. Thumbelina watched him fly away. Tears filled her eyes for she loved the swallow very much.

"Tweet, Tweet!" sang the swallow one last time before it disappeared into the green forest.

Thumbelina was very sad. She never saw the sun, for the wheat around the field mouse's house grew very high. So high that it seemed a thick forest for a girl who was no bigger than a thumb.

"This summer, you must prepare your trousseau!" said the fiel mouse. For the neighbor, that boring mole, had asked for Thumbelina's hand in

marriage. "You are going to need linen. You will be needing sheets and covers when you go to live there."

The field mouse put Thumbelina behind her spinning wheel. The mole came to visit every evening. He kept talking about the future, when the summer would be over and the sun would not be so hot anymore and make the earth hard as rock. Yes, when the summer was over, they would celebrate their wedding.

Thumbelina was not rejoicing, she did not at all like the dull old mole. Every morning at sunrise, and every evening at sunset, she slipped outside. When the wheat swayed a little in the wind, she was able to see the blue sky. She remembered then how wonderful life was up there, among the birds and the flowers. She missed her swallow and would have loved to see him again. But he never came back.

When springtime came again, the swallow said goodbye to Thumbelina.

101

He must be flying over the green forest, far away from her.

When fall came, Thumbelina had finished all her sewing.

"In four weeks, we shall celebrate your wedding!" said the field mouse.

Thumbelina started to cry and said that she did not want to marry the boring mole.

"Nonsense!" said the field mouse. "Don't be hardheaded now or I'll get angry with you! You are going to have a very special husband. Even the queen doesn't have such a beautiful fur coat. And he has a well-stocked cellar and a full kitchen. You ought to thank your stars for such a husband!"

The day of Thumbelina's wedding to the mole finally arrived. The mole came to fetch her. She was going to live with him deep underground and never see the warm sunlight anymore, for sunlight was something he hated.

The poor girl was desperate at the thought of never going outside any-

Thumbelina spent all summer sewing her trousseau.

The day of Thumbelina's wedding to the mole finally arrived.

more. While she was still with the field mouse, she wanted to go and say goodby to the sun.

"Farewell, dear sun," she said when she stood outside, and lifted her arms to the blue sky. She made a few steps through the field mouse's garden. The wheat had been harvested and only the dry stumps were covering the field. ·

"Farewell, farewell!" she said, and put her little arms around a flower. "Say goodby for me to the little swallow if you happen to see him!"

"Tweet, tweet," she heard at that very moment above her head.

She looked up, and, yes, it was indeed the little swallow flying by. And he was, oh, so happy to see Thumbelina again. The girl told the bird how she had to marry an old mole and how terrible that was. She also said that from now on she was going to live underground, where the sun never shone.

"The cold winter is on its way," said the swallow. "I'm flying far away, to warm countries. Don't you want to come with me? You could sit on my back! We shall fly away, far from the ugly mole and his dreary house, far

While she was still with the field mouse,
Thumbelina wanted to say goodbye to the sun.

"Yes, I do want to go with you now!" said Thumbelina. And the swallow flew high up to the sky.

106

across the mountains to a warm place where the sun shines even warmer than here. It is always summer there and marvelous flowers bloom. Come, fly with me Thumbelina. You have saved my life once when I was sick and cold in that dark tunnel!"

"Yes, I do want to go with you now," answered Thumbelina and she hopped on the swallow's back. She tied herself with her belt to the largest feather on his back and they flew high up into the air. They flew over woods and lakes and over the highest snow-covered mountains.

Thumbelina shivered in the cold air, but she snuggled comfortably in the warm feathers of the bird. Only her head peeped through, so that she could watch all the marvels below.

They finally arrived in the warm countries. The sky there was twice as high, and green and red grapes grew everywhere. In the woods, lemons and oranges hung on the trees and every-thing smelled of mint and laurel.

Children played in the fields with giant multicolored butterflies. But the swallow flew on and the scenery be-came even more beautiful! Amidst ma-jestic green trees, near a blue lake, they saw an old castle. It was built all of white marble and was resplendent in the sunlight. Old grapevines were wrapped around its high columns, and all the way on top, there were at least a hundred swallows' nests. One of those nests belonged to our swallow.

"There is my house," said the swal-low. "But let me first put you down,

so that you can pick one of these marvelous flowers. Ah, you are going to love it here!"

"How splendid, how splendid!" cheered Thumbelina and clapped her hands merrily.

A big marble column was lying on the ground, broken in three. It must have fallen down a long time ago. Among its fragments bloomed the prettiest little white flowers. The swal-low flew down with Thumbelina and put her on one of the broad leaves. But what was that? Thumbelina's eyes grew wide with amazement! In the heart of a flower was a little boy, white and transparent, as if he were made of glass. He wore a golden crown on his head and had beautiful little wings and... he was no taller than a thumb! In every one of the flowers there lived such a little boy or girl. And this par-ticular boy happened to be their king.

"Oh, my! He is so handsome!" whispered Thumbelina to the swallow. At first, the little king was afraid of the swallow who looked like a giant to him. But when he saw Thumbelina, he forgot his fear and was very happy, for she was the prettiest girl he had ever seen. So he took off his crown and put it on Thumbelina's head. Then, he asked what her name was and if she would marry him. She would become the queen of all flo-wers!

This was quite different from being the wife of an ugly toad or a mole in black fur coat. Blushing, she courtsied and whispered, "With pleasure." Then, many little boys and girls, no bigger than a thumb, came out of the flowers, They were so beautiful, it was a joy to see them. Everyone brought presents for Thumbelina. But the best of all were the two small white wings. They were fastened on Thumbelina's back, and like the others, she could now fly from flower to flower.

Everybody was merry! The little swallow sat in his nest above, and sang for her as sweetly as only he knew how. But in his heart, he was also a little sad, for he loved Thumbelina so much. He would have liked to stay with her forever.

The king of the flowers put his crown on Thumbelina's head.

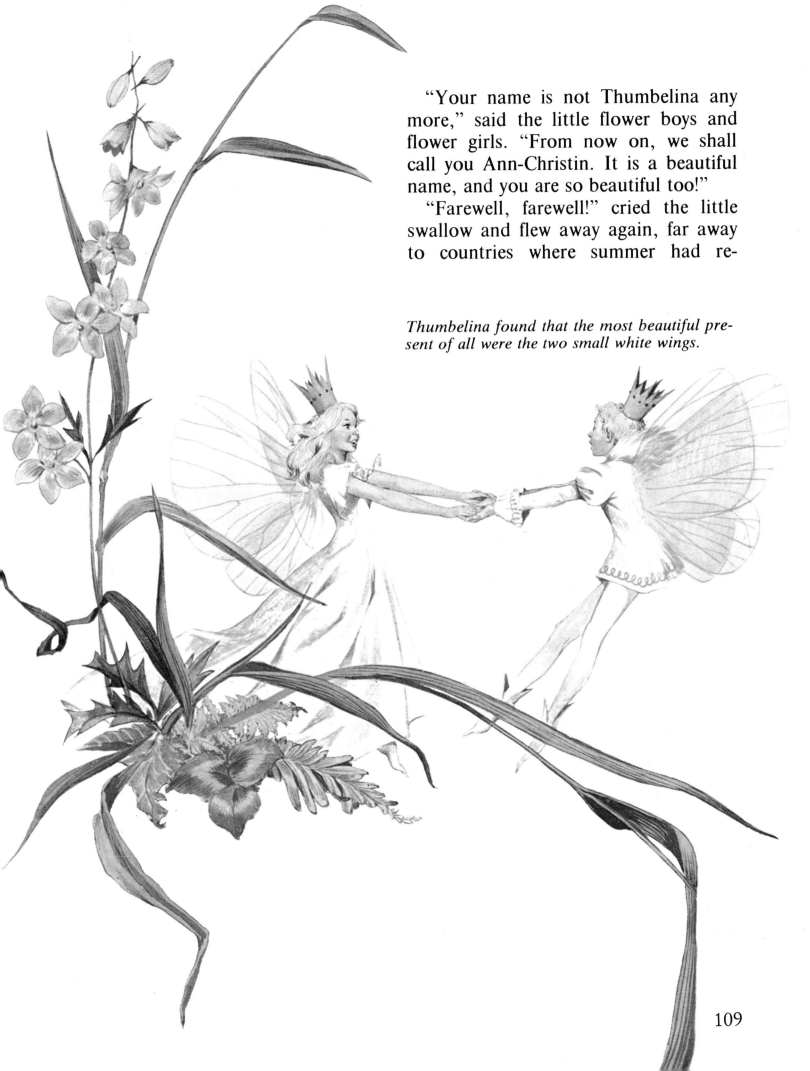

"Your name is not Thumbelina any more," said the little flower boys and flower girls. "From now on, we shall call you Ann-Christin. It is a beautiful name, and you are so beautiful too!"

"Farewell, farewell!" cried the little swallow and flew away again, far away to countries where summer had re-

Thumbelina found that the most beautiful present of all were the two small white wings.

"Farewell, farewell," cried the little swallow and flew away again.

turned once more. In one of those countries the swallow has a nest above the window of someone who can tell beautiful fairy tales. That is where the swallow is right now, and he sings for the one who told us this charming story.

It is Perfectly True

"What a horrible story!" said a hen and shuddered. Yet, the hen who said that lived all the way at the other end of the village where it had all happened.

"What a horrible story!" said the hen once more. "To think that such a thing can happen in a hen house! It is lucky that we are so many here, otherwise I would not dare to roost tonight."

Then the hen told everybody what she had heard. The other hens' feathers stood on end and the cock let his comb droop with fright.

It all began at the other end of the village in a large hen house.

Everybody knows that hens go up to roost around the time when the sun goes down. As usual, on that particular evening, the hens got ready for the night and went to roost.

There was a white hen among them who was always careful to lay her eggs on time and was generally very well mannered. It was, so to speak, a prim and proper hen. As she flew up to the perch, she lost a little white feather.

"Oh," said the white hen, "I lost a feather! But it's all right. The fewer feathers I have, the prettier I'll be."

She said that jokingly, for even if she was very prim and proper and never talked nonsense, she still liked to say a little joke now and then. And without further thought for the lost

112

Among them was a white hen who was very well mannered.

feather, she buried her head under her wing and went to sleep.

Meanwhile the sun had gone down completely and it was dark and quiet in the coop. The hens had nestled close to each other and were all deeply asleep. All? Well, all but one, for one hen was still wide awake. She could not sleep because she kept thinking of the white hen's last words. How was that again? Did she really want to get rid of all her feathers in order to look prettier? How could that be? The sleepless hen found that it was a strange idea. Softly, she nudged her neighbor and whispered,

"Did you hear what the fat white hen said before going to sleep? She wants to pull out all her feathers to make herself more beautiful!! If I were the cock, I wouldn't want her in the hen house anymore."

Right above the hen house lived an owl family. And as everybody probably knows, owls have very sharp ears. They had heard everything that was said down below.

Mother Owl rolled her eyes and fluttered her wings.

"Children," she said, "you should never listen to such nonsense. Your mother doesn't either. But you couldn't help hearing it! Wouldn't you die of shame....? There is a hen below who has no manners! It is not a fit thing for a hen to do, to pluck all her feathers in the presence of a cock.... Simply scandalous!"

"Prenez-garde aux enfants," said Father Owl. Before he came to our

The owl flew to an oak tree in the farmyard where her neighbor lived.

country to get married, he had lived in France for years. So when he wanted to tell his wife something the children should not hear, he said it in French.

Mind the children, that was what he said.

But Mother Owl found the story much too exciting to keep to herself. "I must go and tell this to our neighbor," she said. "She's such a wise owl. She will certainly have an opinion about this!"

She flew to an old oak tree in the farmyard where her neighbor had her nest.

"Ooo, ooohooo," hooted the two lady owls with indignation, after Mother Owl had told her neighbor the story.

"Have you ever heard such a thing?" they asked the doves in the dovecote, who, strangely enough, were still awake. "Have you ever heard such a thing? How scandalous! The white hen in the coop has pulled out all her feathers because she thinks that the cock will find her more attractive that way! But she is so cold now that she is freezing to death. Ooohooo, hoo!"

"In what hen house did it happen?" asked the doves.

"At the neighbor's farm!" said Mother Owl. "I practically saw it with my own eyes. It is not a nice thing to tell, but it is perfectly true!!!"

"Of course it's true, we believe you," said the doves, and called to the rooster,

"You must listen to this! At the neighbor's farm, there is a hen, actually, there are two hens, who pulled out all their feathers. They did it to get noticed, because they want the cock's attention. They believe that he'll find them more attractive than the other hens that way. But it's a dangerous fashion, to start plucking all your feathers like that, for winter is coming soon, and it will be stone-cold. The two hens can very easily catch a cold, then get a fever, or simply freeze to death! We heard that they were actu-

The doves embellished the story in their own way.

ally dead already! Tss, that's how it goes.... Two fine hens, and they died only because they decided to pull out all their feathers!"

The doves had embellished the story in their own way!

"Awake! Awake!" crowed the rooster, very frightened by the doves' account. He flew onto the roof of the chicken coop and called again,

"Awake and listen! In a nearby hen house, there were three hens who died of lovesickness for the cock! They pulled out all their feathers! I find this such a heartbreaking story, that I feel it is my duty to tell it on! How can a cock be so heartless! Doesn't he know that he must divide his attention equally among all hens? What a shame! It was bound to happen sooner or later. Please tell it on! Cucka-dooodle dooo!"

"Tell it on, tell it on!" piped the bats, as they told the story to the nighthawsk. The nighthawk flew on and spoke to all the animals who wanted to hear.

"Pass it on, tell all the hens of the village!" cried the animals. "They must all know about it."

So, the tale went from hen house to hen house, through the whole village and even further.

And it finally came back to the hen house where the white hen lived, the one who had lost a small feather. As you see, the tale had been retold over and over again. And everybody had embellished it a little by adding to it. Finally, the story was changed so much that the hens were not aware that it had all started with themselves. This is how the story came back to them: "I have heard that five hens from the village all fell in love with the same cock. They all lost a lot of weight, and to prove who was the slimmest, they pulled out all their feathers. When the cock, who was to pick the winner, decided that they

were all equally thin, they went mad. They started pecking each other till they were covered with blood. Not one hen survived. They are all dead! What a shame for the hens, and also, what a shame for the owner!"

The white hen who had lost one tiny little feather did not realize that it had all happened because she had once said in jest, "The fewer feathers I have, the prettier I'll be."

And since the white hen was prim and proper, and had good manners, she also said,

"How scandalous! And those hens aren't the only ones who behave so badly! How can a hen act that way only because she's in love with a cock? What is more, pulling all your feathers won't get you anywhere. This story should not be hushed up. We have to pass it on, so that all hens can hear it. Such a thing must never happen again!"

That is what the white hen said.

The story was told on and on, till all the animals in the country knew it.

One little feather can grow to become five hens! Yes, it is perfectly true!

„Cuckadooodle dooo! Pass it on! Cuckadooodle dooo!"

117

Five Peas in a Pod

Once upon a time there were five peas, all in one pod. The peas were nice and green, and the pod was green too! So, naturally, they thought that the whole world must be green. And they were right, of course. . . . as far as their little world was concerned. But you know that there are many more colors in the world, and many are far prettier than the color green.

But the little peas could not even imagine that, for they had never seen anything beyond their tiny green pea pod world.

And what did they see when they looked around?

They saw their little brothers and sisters, who were all of the same green color! And they saw the walls of their pea pod house, and the walls were

green too. That is why all the peas were convinced that the whole world had to be green.

The weather outside was beautiful and the rays of the golden sun warmed their green pod. The light shone through the green walls of the pod and the peas said to each other,

"Look at the green sunshine! Isn't it so nice and warm?"

That's how you think when you are a green pea, who cannot see any further than his own pea pod.

Days went by and the peas lived happily in their little green world. They couldn't see that their pod grew in the middle of the king's garden, that was the most enchanting garden in the whole country. And they did not realize that they were surrounded

Every pea had his own little place, in a neat row.

by a rainbow of bright colors, resplendent in the sunshine. The king's palace was made of the purest white marble, with golden towers, and all the doors and windows were painted bright red. There were at least a hundred gardeners working in the palace and they had planted the most precious flowers in the king's garden. Altogether there must have been a hundred colors there! There were red roses, blue violets, yellow tulips, pink carnations, purple asters, orange marygolds, and many more flowers of all shapes and colors. There was a big blue pond in the center of the garden, and swimming in the pond, there were six graceful white swans. But the little peas had never seen all those wonders and they were saying, "How nice it is here, in our green pod, and how delighted we are with our green world!"

And, in the beginning, they did have a great life. The pod was small, but then, so were the peas. Everyone had his own place in a neat row.

When the sun started to shine on their little green bodies, they began to grow.

Summer came and when the sun started to shine on their little green bodies, they began to grow. The pod grew along with them, so there was always enough room for all five of them. They were comfortable and everything was comfortable in their pod. It was kept warm and cozy by the sunshine, and when it became too hot, the soft summer rain fell to make it nice and cool again. Life was exactly as it should be. During the day, there was light and when night fell, it was dark. It was never too hot or too cold, and with all that, they grew like cabbages, though they were only peas, of course.

But as they grew up and became almost adults, the peas started to wonder what they were going to do with their lives.

"We can't just spend the rest of our life sitting here in a pod," said the largest pea. "I am beginning to feel stiff from sitting still all day!" said the middle one.

"I wouldn't be surprised if something happened soon!" said the smallest pea. "Somehow, I have the feeling that the world is going to change for us."

But changes in the world happen very slowly, and it took many weeks

"The world is shaking," said the peas to each other.

before something actually changed. Only, the coming change was going to be a very important one. Slowly, the peas became yellow, and their pea pod became yellow too.

"Look at this! Now the whole world is turning yellow!" they said, and they were right again. For someone who couldn't see beyond the limit of his pod, everything was yellow indeed.

Then one day, the peas suddenly felt a shock. They felt themselves roughly shaken. It was a good thing that every little pea was sitting tight in his place, or they would have rolled all over each other and got all mixed up. And it would have been quite confusing, for in the world everything belongs in its right place, and has to stay there.

"The world is shaking!" they exclaimed. Once more, it wasn't quite correct. Only their pod was shaking, along with a few others on

The peas were very excited to see what would happen next.

the same vine. A big human hand had plucked them and stuffed them in a jacket pocket.

"Something is going to happen soon!" they said to each other. "Maybe our pod is going to open." They sat in their places and waited anxiously.

"I am curious to see which one of us will go farthest." said the little pea.

"We shall soon find out." said the second one.

"Don't fret, everything will happen as it is supposed to happen" said the biggest of them all.

The man who had picked the pods was the forest keeper of the palace, and every time he came by the garden and passed the pea patch, he would pluck a pea pod for his youngest son. In his room, the forest keeper's son had a miniature fortress with real tin soldiers and a real little cannon. He used the peas that his father brought him, as cannonballs.

And that day, when his father came

home, he brought some more peas for his little son's cannon.

The peas heard a loud crack! The pod had burst open and all five of them rolled out of their neat little spots, and into the hand of the little boy.

"These peas are just what I need for my cannon," said the little boy.

For the first time in their life they were in full sunlight.

"Wow, look at this! The world has become completely golden!" they exclaimed. And again, they were convinced that it was the reality.

The forest keeper's son examined each pea carfully.

"These will be just perfect for my cannon," he said as he placed one into the barrel and shot it off.

"Farewell, my friends! I am flying off into the wide world! Catch me if you can!" cried the pea before he disappeared.

"I am going to fly straight up, all the way to the sun," said the second pea. "The sun is made of real gold, and it lives in a golden world. A nice warm place like that is just the perfect spot for me."

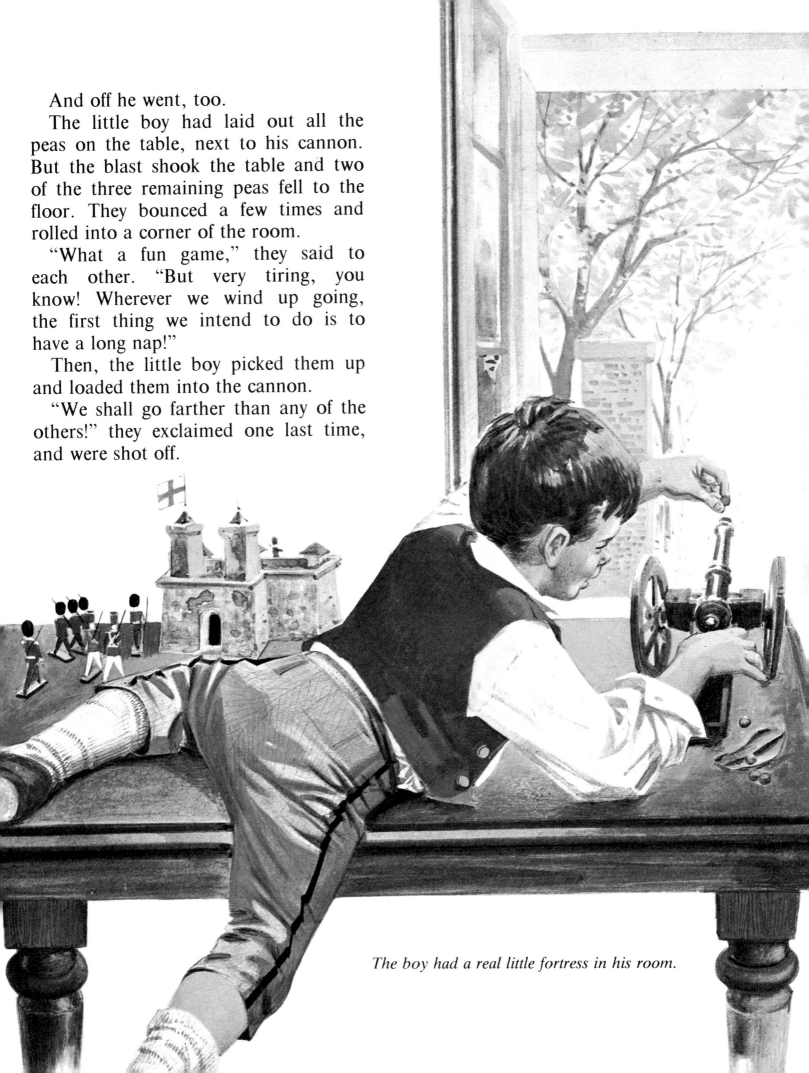

And off he went, too.

The little boy had laid out all the peas on the table, next to his cannon. But the blast shook the table and two of the three remaining peas fell to the floor. They bounced a few times and rolled into a corner of the room.

"What a fun game," they said to each other. "But very tiring, you know! Wherever we wind up going, the first thing we intend to do is to have a long nap!"

Then, the little boy picked them up and loaded them into the cannon.

"We shall go farther than any of the others!" they exclaimed one last time, and were shot off.

The boy had a real little fortress in his room.

"Whatever will be, will be." said the fifth pea.

Finally, he too was shot from the cannon and flew very far away. He went all the way to a little old cottage. He hit a board, just below the attic window and got embedded in a crack filled with moss. The soft moss closed around the pea, and it lay there, completely hidden from sight.

"Whatever will be, will be." he said once more.

In the little attic room lived a very poor woman. Every morning she got up early and went into the village, where she cleaned stoves, chopped firewood, did the washing and all kinds of chores for the rich families who lived there. Fortunately the woman was still young and strong enough to do hard work and earn a living, though it wasn't much of a living, she still remained very poor.

Her daughter lived with her in the little attic room, and every night she waited for her mother to come home from work. The daughter was a young and very pretty girl, but she had been sick for more than a year and wasn't getting any better. She was very pale and her mother was afraid that she might die any day.

"I fear that one of these days she is going to go to heaven, to join her sister," thought the woman. "I had two daughters and it has always been so difficult for me to take care of them since their father died. We were always so poor that even finding two dresses and two pairs of shoes for them was more than I could manage. But in spite of it all I was so happy to have my little girls. When my older

The peas rolled into a corner of the room.

one became sick, I worked twice as hard, I did everything I could for her. And yet, she still died and I know her sweet young soul is in heaven now. Sometimes, at night, when I look up to the sky, I'm sure I can see her pretty little face among the stars. And maybe she looks at us too and wants her sister to join her up there so that they can play together with the fluffy white clouds and the silvery stars."

The little girl did not die, but her health was not improving either. Day after day, she just lay there waiting for her mother to come home from the village at night, and days seemed very long to her. But she lay there pa-tiently and invented all kinds of games to take her through the endless boring days. Sometimes she closed her eyes and imagined that she was lying in a beautiful room in a gigantic palace, surrounded by servants and ladies-in-waiting. But when she opened her eyes again, she saw nothing more than her dreary attic room and the grey mouse whom she fed bread crumbs every now and then, and the little bird sitting on a branch outside her window and singing for her. Another time, she imagined that she was sun bathing in a magnificent garden, filled with the most beautiful flowers, red roses, blue violets, yellow tulips and pink carnations, purple asters and orange mary-

In the little attic room lived a very poor woman.

golds. . . They all grew in the gardens of a king! And there were snow-white swans swimming about in a blue pond. Her own little bed had been placed on a boat, and she was lying there, lulled by the clear water, admiring all the bright flowers that surrounded her.

A whole year had gone by since the peas had left their pod and were shot from the little boy's cannon.

All kinds of birds came to sing for the little sick girl.

Sometimes she imagined that she was lying in a big room in a magnificent palace.

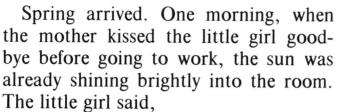

Spring arrived. One morning, when the mother kissed the little girl good-bye before going to work, the sun was already shining brightly into the room. The little girl said,

"Mother, I noticed something green that looks as if it grew out there, under the lowest window pane. Look how it sways in the breeze, that must be a little plant from my garden!"

"But, dear child, we do not have a

The woman chopped fire wood...

garden! If I had a little money, I would buy a window box and grow flowers in it for you, but unfortunately, I have no money at all. The winter has been so long and so cold."

"No, no, Mother, I am sure that there is something green out there, please, go and find out!" insisted the little girl. With a sigh, her mother went to open the window.

"Good heavens, you are right!" she said surprised. "It is a little plant, but how can a plant just appear out of nowhere? She bent a little more over the windowsill and realized what it

....and did the washing.

131

was, "It is a pea that sprouted through the moss," she said. "Now at last, you have a little plant to look at!"

"This will be the first plant in my garden." said the little girl, and she smiled at the fragile little stem with its small green leaves.

The mother put her daughter's bed close by the window so that she could watch her plant. Then she went off to work.

When she came back that evening, it seemed to her that her sick little girl was looking a little better.

"Mother, I have been lying in the sun all day, and it was so nice," she

"You are right," said her mother, "it is a little plant indeed!"

said. "And I'm almost sure that the little pea has grown at least half an inch today. I am going to try very hard to become as strong as my pea plant. It has spent all winter outside, waiting for spring to come and bring along the warm sunshine. And I too have been lying here all winter long, waiting. Now we shall grow strong together, my little pea plant and I, a little more every day, until I recover completely and can go outside and walk in the sun."

"Ah, what I would give to see the day when you become healthy again!"

said her mother, but she was afraid that it would almost be too much to hope for.

To keep the fragile pea plant from being broken by the wind, the mother tied it to a little stick with a piece of string. Then she ran a line to the window frame so that the vine had something to climb on, if it should ever grow that big. Every day she watered the pea plant that had become very important for her because, through its own fragile green life, it had given her daughter the will to get better.

And the pea plant kept growing, encouraged by the sunshine and the care of the sick little girl and her mother. They could see that it was getting bigger every day.

"Well, look at this!" the woman said one morning as she went to water the plant. "It is growing little flowers now! Who would ever have thought that the tiny little pea could alive without so much as a garden or even a flowerpot? It just thrives here, in a few inches of moss, it grows into a beautiful plant, and now it even gives us flowers! How marvelous nature is!"

Somehow, it made her begin to believe that her little daughter had a chance to recover, for she was looking better every day. She was taking pride

The little girl looked better every day.

in what she called her garden, and was talking more and more excitedly about it. Right now, it was no more than a pea plant, but in her dreams, it became a big garden, full of the rarest flowers of all colors. The little girl sat in her bed and gazed happily at her one-pea-plant-garden.

The following week, the little girl was already able to stay up for an hour or so. Summer was already there, and the warm air came through the wide open window. Her mother put a chair nearby, so that she could rest in it.

With shining eyes, the little girl sat by the window and watched her plant.

When she finally got up for the first time, the little girl was mad with joy. She was still frail and a bit pale, but she sat by the attic window with shining eyes, and all day she watched the pea plant which by now had grown into a big bush. She leaned over and kissed the little white flowers. The soft rays of the warm summer sun caressed her hair. That first day will always be remembered as a day of celebration by both the mother and the daughter!

Her mother said, "Nature, which made this little pea grow, took care of it through the dark, cold winter. You were very sick, but you too have had the strength to live through the long, cold winter days. The little pea, which was a gift to you from nature, has grown into a beautiful plant by now. You too will grow up to become a

Summer was there!

137

handsome and healthy young woman and you'll be just as strong as any other girl in the village. As she spoke, there were tears of gratefulness and joy in the mother's eyes. She smiled at her daughter and they both looked at the little pea flowers.

"I still don't understand how the pea could have found its way to this crack in the beam," said the mother.

"Oh, I do, I understand very well," answered the girl with a smile. "It was meant for me, the pea had to be the first plant in my garden. Really, it is a gift from heaven!"

Meanwhile, let us see what has happened to the other peas from the same pod. Well, the first pea, who had cried "Catch me if you can!"

when he flew out into the wide world, landed in a gutter, and was quickly caught. . . and eaten by a pigeon. The two lazy peas, who had said that the first thing they were going to do was sleep, regardless of where they landed, did not go too far. Another pigeon picked them and fed them to his young.

Pea number four, who wanted to go all the way to the sun, only wound up in a gutter, like the first one. There he stayed, for days and weeks. The water in the gutter made him swell up till he was three times as big as before. "Im becoming nice and fat, and so handsome!" he said. 'I only hope that I don't burst. I am sure that there is no other pea in the whole world who can

How nice and fat I am getting,"
said the pea.

manage to get as fat as I! I don't know what happened to the others from my pod, but I'm sure that I am the most special of all!"

Now we know what happened to each of them, and we realize that it was really the fifth pea who had most reason to feel proud of himself. For that pea had made a big difference in somebody's life. He had made a little girl and her hard working mother very happy. The girl now stood by her attic window. Her eyes were bright and she had a healthy color on her cheeks, you could see how happy she was to be healthy at last, after so many years. With her soft gentle hands, she caressed every little pea flower. Now she had no doubt that one day she would have a real garden of her own, full of pea plants and flowers of all sizes and colors!

The little girl caressed the pea flowers with her gentle hands.

The Princess
and the Pea

The prince traveled around the whole world to find a real pricess.

Once upon a time there was a prince who wanted very much to marry a princess. Only . . . . it had to be a real princess.

He traveled around the whole world to find one but there was always something wrong.

Not that there weren't enough princesses around, but one could never be sure that they were real. There was always a little something that gave the prince reasons to be suspicious.

So, he finally became disillusioned and returned to his castle, wondering whether he would be able to marry a real princess.

One evening, there was a terrible storm raging over the kingdom. It brought flashes of lightning with roaring thunder and a torrential downpour.

Somebody knocked at the castle door.

The old king went down to open. Before him was a princess, but what a sorry sight she was! She was soaked through and her blond hair was all undone!

The water dripped down her clothes and made a puddle where she stood on the floor.

The rain came in through the tip of

There was a princess at the door, but what a sorry sight she was!

her shoes and came out again through the back. And yet. . . . she was a real princess, she said.

The king took her to see the queen.

"We shall soon find out whether she is a real princess or not!" thought the old queen. Without saying a word, she went to prepare the guest room.

There, she took off the mattress and all the sheets from the bed. At the bottom of the bed she placed a pea and covered it with many mattresses.

She then put quite as many down quilts on top of the mattresses.

The princess was to spend the night on this high pile of soft mattresses and down quilts.

The following morning at breakfast, the queen asked the princess if she had slept well.

"Oh, Dear! I'm afraid not!" said the princess. "I have hardly been able to sleep at all! Heaven knows what there was in my bed, but it was something very hard for I am black and blue all over! A horrible night indeed!"

That is how the king and the queen knew that she was a real princess. Through all the thick mattresses and the soft down quilts, she had still felt the tiny little pea!

Only the skin of a princess can be so sensitive.

So the prince married her because at last he was certain that he would have a real princess for a wife.

The pea was put in a glass jewel box and exhibited in a museum. It is still there to this day, unless of course, somebody took it away.

The princess spent the night on a pile of mar-
velously soft mattresses and down quilts.

© 1976 by Gruppo Editoriale Fabbri S.p.A., Milan

Published by Blitz Editions
an imprint of Bookmart Limited
Registered Number 2372865
Trading as Bookmart Limited
Desfort Road
Enderby
Leicester
LE9 5AD

ISBN 1 85605 116 1

Illustrations by Maraja, Michele, Pikka, Sani, Sergio, Una

Printed in Italy by Gruppo Editoriale Fabbri S.p.A., Milan